Love's Misfiring Magic

Wildcrest Witches Book 1

HEATHER SILVIO

Panther Books

BOOKS BY HEATHER SILVIO

PARANORMAL TALENT AGENCY
(ALSO IN LARGE PRINT)

Lights, Camera, Action (Episode One)
Reset to One (Episode Two)
That's a Wrap (Episode Three)
An Unexpected Sequel (Episode Four)
Jumping the Shark (Episode Five)
The Season Finale (Episode Six)

COLLECTIONS

Paranormal Talent Agency Episodes 1-3 Collection
Paranormal Talent Agency Episodes 4-6 Collection
Paranormal Talent Agency Episodes 1-6 Collection

DOCTOR DANGER MYSTERIES

Hazard in Hawaii

NON-SERIES FICTION

Not Quite Famous: A Romantic Comedy of an Actress
on the Edge
Beyond the Abyss: Tales of the Supernatural
Courting Death

NONFICTION

Special Snowflake Syndrome: The Unrecognized
Personality Disorder Destroying the World

Happiness by the Numbers: 9 Steps to Authentic
Happiness

Stress Disorders: A Healing Path for PTSD

CHAPTER ONE

SHELLY

Shelly Newsome's goal tonight had been to win back her ex-boyfriend, not send him to the emergency room. Yet, there they were. At least the six-story sprawling Wildcrest Hospital complex was state-of-the-art. That was thanks to Mia Fynn filming her movie about witches here. When it became one of the highest-grossing films of all time, map-dot-sized Wildcrest experienced a boom in tourism. The fact that the town, located in the wilds of Nevada, actually provided a safe haven for supernatural beings met the definition of exquisite irony in Shelly's book.

If only the doctor would stop looking like he was trying not to laugh. He avoided making eye contact, no doubt because that would push him over the comical edge. Shelly sighed. Of course, Dr. Benjamin Wright was her best friend, so she supposed it was only natural.

"I don't know what happened," Shelly said, pacing a circle on the bland linoleum between two rows of plastic chairs, trying not to let the beige walls close in. "It wasn't a complicated spell, I didn't think." Her history with spell-making was by no means stellar. But she meant what she said to Ben. "I'm not sure what went wrong." Anxiety zinged through her, the taste of bile in the back of her mouth. "You're sure he's going to be all right? The way that he grabbed his throat, struggled to breathe." She suddenly had a hard time catching her breath.

"Breathe, Shelly."

She inhaled, held to a four count, exhaled. Repeated. Ignored the scent of noxious hospital disinfectant that threatened to overwhelm her nasal passages. Ignored the buzzing of her cellphone in her pocket. She knew it was her mother calling. Again. "Thanks. I've never seen someone turn that shade of purple." The blood drained from her face. "I could have killed him."

"You didn't." Ben leaned in and lowered his voice. "I knew he'd be okay when they brought him in. You never had anything to worry about."

"Thank the Goddess." She breathed a sigh of relief. All witches' magic had specific inclinations that typically surfaced during puberty. Ben's ability was to sense the physical health of others – both good and bad – and intuitively know what they needed, whether traditional or magical intervention. So, if he said Ethan was never in any real danger, Shelly believed him. If only she could get a grasp on her own magical aptitude.

Ben's cellphone buzzed and he raised his eyebrows at her when he saw the caller.

Of course, her mother was calling Ben. Shelly gave a small shake of her head. She'd call her mother back when everything felt more settled.

"I guess what they say isn't true, that a way to a man's heart is through his stomach," Ben said, and now he outright laughed, the sound bouncing around the small, thankfully empty, waiting area. Shelly refrained from reading him the riot act. When you've known someone your entire life – and were best friends since he took the blame for a minor car accident in high school even though it was your fault – you cut them a little slack. A little.

"Gee, thanks. That's very supportive." She collapsed into one of the green plastic waiting room chairs, dropped her head into her hands. "What if I'd seriously hurt him?" She mumbled through her fingers.

"Look at me," Ben said. She didn't. "Shelly Newsome, look at me right now. Please."

Shelly raised her head, her hazel eyes meeting his brown ones. "At least you said please."

"Tell me what happened."

Horror filled her as tears flowed. Ben's smirk fell and he pulled Shelly into a hug. She leaned into the embrace, her hands clutching at his familiar scrubs. Warmth enveloped her. He held her until the tears slowed then stopped. "Ethan broke up with me this morning," she muttered into Ben's shoulder. "He says he's moving out at the end of the month. In five days."

Ben pushed Shelly to arm's length, eyes wide in shock. "He broke up with you? Why didn't you tell me sooner? And why were you baking him a magical dinner if he's leaving in five days?"

She broke eye contact. "This morning, I thought… I thought he was going to propose," she whispered.

"Oh, Shelly."

"Yeah, yeah, I know."

"Didn't you tell me you thought something was missing?" Ben asked, confusion clear on his face. He ran a hand through his short brown hair.

A flush crept up Shelly's neck. "Let me explain." She fiddled with the bottom of her t-shirt, rubbing the soft cotton fabric. "I thought what was missing was me hiding the witch side of myself from him."

Prior to *Witches in the Wild* filming there years ago, the supernatural beings in town mostly kept that quiet. Once the movie shot to success, they could live openly to a certain extent because the normals and the tourists thought they were playing up the movie angle for tourist dollars.

That wasn't entirely wrong, of course, but the tongue-in-cheek approach had masked the truth. And, then once the Las Vegas city council officially recognized the existence of supernaturals last year, even more beings decided to live openly. Shelly had chosen not to share her witch nature with Ethan in part because she didn't identify as a witch. Why would she when she couldn't cast basic spells?

"I thought that when he proposed," Shelly continued, "the promise of taking our relationship to the next level would give me the prompt to tell him the truth."

"Why did you think he was going to propose?"

She tilted her head back, long black hair hitting the seat bottom. "He said he had something important to talk to me about." She shrugged. "After five years together, what else could it be?"

"He broke up with you instead."

"Yep."

"Now I'm even more confused. If he broke up with you this morning, why would you be making him—" He stopped with a shake of his head.

He knew her too well.

"You were trying to win him back." He grimaced when she nodded. "But why?"

"He's the one."

"Even though there's no spark?"

"Yes." Shelly picked at her cuticles. "It's a slow-build relationship."

Ben snorted.

"All right, I get it. Five years is a long time to build."

"What happened at dinner? I assume you weren't trying a love spell."

"Of course not!" All witches knew that love spells were verboten. Free will didn't allow for that. But that didn't mean they couldn't nudge other directions. Her brow furrowed. "I was making vegetable lasagna, his favorite meal. I wanted to make sure that the positive feelings were as strong as possible, so I added saffron to ensure a good mood, plus included a magical enhancement. To boost it."

Ben's eyes twinkled. "That explains his symptoms."

"I'm so glad," she said with an eye roll.

"No need to be sarcastic."

"Sorry. I know you're trying to help."

He thought for a moment. "Interesting that Ben had the exact opposite response. Sadness, irritability, asthma attack."

Now Shelly gave him the side eye. "Uh huh, I get it."

"I just find it interesting that your magical enhancement worked in the opposite direction," he repeated with a shrug.

"Why can't I be a better witch?" Shelly groused.

Ben half-smiled. "I don't know. Maybe the Goddess was trying to tell you something."

"That I shouldn't cast spells," she said, defeated.

Ben closed the space between them and opened his mouth to speak, but another voice overrode his.

"Shelly, honey. Is everything okay? Jenny from book club called to tell me she saw you in the ER."

Ah, the beauty of the small town. Shelly stood to face the owner of the husky voice. "Hi, Mom."

CHAPTER TWO

BEN

Ben's jaw had snapped shut at the sound of Grace Newsome's voice; she commanded whatever space she entered. After she passed the final row of chairs in the small room, he joined Shelly in embracing her mother, awed as always that someone's mother could be so cool.

Not that Ben didn't love his mother, but she was quieter and laser-focused on the family business, Wildcrest Witches International. Yep, their family business was running the coven's corporate entity. Welcome to the 21st century of practicing witchcraft. They even considered taking the business public after Las Vegas passed their resolution, but thankfully, that impulse passed. His mother, the Chief Financial Officer, wasn't a witch, but her facility with numbers was nearly magical.

"Shelly, Ben, I'm glad I found you both," Grace said into Ben's chest. She was short like her daughter, but rail thin where Shelly had curves that made a man want to— He slammed that line of thinking down and concentrated on the firebrand before them.

"Hi Grace, we're fine, as you can see," he assured her, worry lines clear on her face.

Grace shook her head, causing the halo of shoulder-length curly red hair to bounce around her face and her dangling earrings to jangle. "Thank the Goddess. When Jenny called, and neither of you answered your phones, it was all I could do to contain myself." Her purple eyes filled with tears. When Ben was in high school, he'd assumed those were contacts, but no, her eyes were purple. Shelly explained that the color related to her mother's magical inclination to recognize the happiness potential of others.

Shelly and Ben exchanged a guilty look. They'd both seen her mother's calls, but the woman could be excitable, and they had wanted to make sure that Ethan was good first.

"I'm so sorry, Mom," Shelly said, hugging her mother again. "But, Ben's right. You can see we're fine." She swallowed. "Though Ethan is being treated."

"Is he okay?" Grace asked, politely, as if discussing a stranger.

"He's going to be perfectly fine," Ben answered the question. "He'll be released in about an hour." Had Shelly told her they'd broken up? He'd always wondered what Grace thought of Shelly's boyfriend – ex-boyfriend. She never seemed fond of him. Or maybe that was wishful thinking on his part.

"What happened?" Grace asked.

Shelly placed her hand on his upper arm. "I'll explain it, Ben." She stared at the ceiling for a moment. "Ethan reacted to a spell."

"What did you do?" Grace managed to ask the question without sounding accusatory at all.

Shelly still reddened. "I was trying to increase his feelings of wellbeing."

"Let me guess? It did the opposite."

"How did you know?"

Shelly's mother leaned into the green plastic chair next to her, fingers wrapping over the top. "When your magical abilities first manifested, that happened all the time."

"Why don't I remember that it did the opposite?"

Grace's fingernails tapped out a staccato beat on the chair back. "I have no idea."

"Wait. Is that why you bound my magic until I graduated high school?" Shelly's voice definitely sounded accusatory. "I thought it was because you wanted it to mature." Now, she sounded sad. Ben's heart ached for her.

"Can't both of those things be true?" Grace asked with a tilt of her head.

Emotions played across Shelly's face as she considered her mother's question. Then the uncertainty cleared and her grin lit the room. Ben smiled automatically in response. Her ability to remain positive had always drawn him to her.

"Yeah, for sure," Shelly agreed with her mother. "Guess it didn't work as well as we'd hoped. Do you think it'll mature by the time I'm thirty?"

Grace shrugged. "Darling, I have no idea."

"Do you want to see Ethan?" Shelly asked.

"Of course," she answered, though again Ben noted a lack of genuine interest. Hmm.

"Let me know when he's ready to be discharged, so I can take him home," Shelly said to Ben, her voice hitching on the final word. Grace's eyes narrowed in response.

He assured Shelly he would, then watched the women exit the public side of the waiting area, weaving past the rows of empty chairs toward the automatic sliding glass doors. Grace's flowing patchwork skirt swirled around her legs and Shelly's jeans did wonderful things for her backside. Someone snickering behind him caught his attention. Ben turned to face the man standing in the doorway of the medical staff entrance.

"Can I help you, nurse?" Ben asked in his most condescending doctor voice. The owner of the snicker belly laughed.

"When are you going to tell Shelly you've got it bad for her?" Nick Moore asked, mischief in his dark blue eyes.

Ben sighed. "It's complicated."

"Dude, you've wanted her since high school. It's time to uncomplicate it."

"Yeah, and I've been in the Friend Zone since high school," he reminded Nick.

"That's entirely your fault. You had many opportunities."

"Not hardly. She dated what's-his-name, Will, all through high school, then moved away from Wildcrest to go to college," Ben said, as though Nick, his best male friend, didn't remember all of that. The supernatural support found in their tiny corner of Nevada meant that few left. Those who did invariably returned.

"Ancient history, my man," Nick disagreed.

"And then she met Ethan senior year of college. I still can't believe he agreed to move here with her when they graduated," Ben said. "You'd think our small town was too small for the city slicker."

"C'mon, Ben. Ethan's not a bad guy. You know that," Nick said.

Ben cringed. Nick was right. Just because Ethan had what Ben wanted – and threw it away. "This stays between us," Ben said in a lower voice, "but Shelly told me Ethan broke up with her this morning."

"Now's your chance!"

"I started to, but then Grace arrived."

"Fine. When you get Shelly alone again, now's your chance." He enunciated the repeated phrase.

Ben hesitated.

"What?" Nick asked in exasperation.

"You know what. What if I say something and lose the friendship?" The thought of not having Shelly in his life…

"What if you say something and she jumps into your arms?"

Ben lifted an eyebrow at the image of Shelly jumping into his arms. "I'm too tall for that," he said with a chuckle.

"Joke all you want," Nick said, then glanced back into the room behind him. Another nurse beckoned to him from near a blue privacy curtain inside one of the half-dozen glassed-off rooms. Nick clasped a hand on Ben's shoulder. "Don't blow this."

CHAPTER THREE

SHELLY

"What's going on, Shelly?" her mother asked when they stepped away from Ben. She stood with her hands on her hips, almost like a petulant child.

Shelly smiled. "What makes you think something is going on?" They had stopped outside the sliding door for Ethan's triage room. Shelly reached to open it, and Grace placed her hand on her daughter's.

"Shelly. Honey. You almost never use your magic. Yet you did tonight. What's going on?"

At the repeated question, Shelly pulled her arm back from the door and hung her head. "Ethan broke up with me." The dam broke. Shelly explained everything that had happened. When she finished, Grace pulled her into a tight hug.

"Oh, darling. I'm sorry." She led her a few steps away from the door to a set of green plastic waiting chairs up against the wall. Shelly idly wondered why every section of the emergency department looked the same to her.

"Thanks, Mom." She perched on the edge of a chair, her leg bouncing.

"How are you feeling now?"

"I'm okay." *How are you supposed to feel when you accidentally nearly kill your recent ex?* Shelly's fingers began tapping out a beat on her bouncing leg.

"Relax, darling. Ben said Ethan will be okay. No harm, no foul."

"This time," she said darkly. "What about next time?"

"Maybe don't try your magic like this?"

"Hmm."

"That's not an insult to your magic," Grace assured her.

"I know, Mom. It's not my… area of strength. I think that's how you've put it with your clients?" Shelly's mother was a life coach for supernaturals. And, apparently quite good at it. Her magical inclination to sense the happiness of others and guide them toward increasing it was a perfect fit for that vocation.

"Have you thought about what you really want?"

"What do you mean?"

"How's your website design freelancing going?"

The unexpected segue caught Shelly off-guard. "Pretty good," she said, a slight stretching of the truth. Okay, that was a lie. Despite her misfiring magic, her magical inclination appeared to be sensing the magic of others and seeing the order in the chaos. Design seemed a good fit, and she was trying to parlay her experience with one of the biggest marketing companies on the west coast into her own small business. Except it'd been slow going. She wasn't about to be homeless or anything that dire, though she was pinching her pennies.

"Prior to the breakup, how was your relationship with Ethan?"

"Pretty good," she said again. But maybe Ben was right. Maybe that missing spark was more of an issue than she was willing to admit.

"What have you learned from your decisions to date?"

"That I'm tenacious?"

"Yes! You go after what you want."

"Okay…"

"That's what you need to do now."

Her mother made that pronouncement with utter conviction, but it confused Shelly. That had been her plan. She was going after what she wanted. Ethan. And it flamed out. Spectacularly. Because she sucked as a witch. Her lips thinned into a line of displeasure. Grace placed her hand on Shelly's still-bouncing leg.

"Just be sure you're going after the right things."

"Is there something you want to tell me?" Despite usually being straightforward, to the point of being blunt, every now and again Grace would speak in riddles like that. Like there was something Shelly was missing. Except, like a good coach, and within the bounds of her magic, she wouldn't give her daughter the answer.

Grace grinned. "I trust you'll do what's best for you." She stood, stretched her arms over her head. "I'm glad everybody's okay, but I'm exhausted. And, I'm sure your father is waiting up."

Shelly glanced at her watch; it was after midnight. "Give Dad a hug for me," she said, standing next to her mother. "Thanks for coming down to check on us."

"I love you, darling."

"Love you, too." Shelly watched Grace walk past the nurses' station in the middle of the room toward the exit, mind racing to uncover the subtext of what she'd been told. She knew her mother. There was definitely subtext. With a sigh, she entered Ethan's room, closing the door behind her.

Her breath caught in her throat at the sight of Ethan Platt, her boy— ex-boyfriend, she corrected herself. Even pale and hooked up to machines monitoring his vital signs, the man was a vision. Blond hair. Cheekbones that could cut glass. Long eyelashes women were envious of, and always commented on... even in front of Shelly. She bristled a little at the memory. He'd shocked her when he'd approached during senior year of college. Shelly was what people called cute; he looked like a Greek god in search of his goddess. He'd turned out to be down to earth though. They'd always gotten along great. Well, until the last year.

Beeping increased on one of the machines, drawing her attention. Ethan's head moved to the side. "Ethan?" She asked softly, in case he wasn't really waking up.

His eyes opened, the blue vivid in his face. "Hey, Shelly. Did I fall asleep?"

"You did. How are you feeling?"

"Much better." His voice was gravelly, but his smile was full wattage. "Ben said I can leave soon?"

"He did. I can take you home?" Asked, rather than assumed.

Ethan's smile slipped a fraction. "That'd be great. A ride back to the apartment."

The word change struck like an arrow to her heart. "Right. The apartment."

"But no more home-cooked meals," he teased, maybe to take the edge off.

It worked. She chuckled. "You got it." She approached the bed, hesitating to touch him. "Let me talk to Ben. I'll be right back," she said brightly, instead.

"That sounds good, thanks." Ethan's eyelids were already drooping.

Guilt surged. She knew it was late, but still, this had to be an aftereffect of her misfired spell. She closed the door gently behind her and set off in search of Ben. A quick search, since he was now reviewing someone's chart at the nurse's station in the center of the room.

"Is that Ethan's chart? He'd like to know if he's cleared for me to take him back to the apartment." It saddened Shelly that she'd already adopted the word change. *What about my mother's recommendation to go after what I wanted?*

"It's not his chart; I've already taken care of it." He gestured to the side. "I believe Nick is wrapping up some final notes before we officially release."

"Thanks, Ben," she said. "You're such a good friend. I don't know what I'd do without you."

His eyes dropped to the chart he was reviewing. "Glad I could help."

"Mom told me I should go after what I want," she blurted out and he met her gaze.

"You always should."

"She also said I should be careful continuing to use my magic."

He quirked an eyebrow.

"Okay, okay, she said not to use my magic."

"That sounds more like it."

"How can I help Ethan see we belong together without magical assistance?" she asked, more to herself than to Ben.

"Ethan's what you want."

Shelly couldn't tell if Ben was asking or agreeing with her, so she chose not to address it. "I know I can't do a love spell. And, even a smaller spell to increase wellbeing misfired. How do I show Ethan I care?"

"Should magic be necessary to show someone you care?"

She waved a hand dismissively. "When time is of the essence, you use what's available to you. I have only five days. Four, really." Ben's expression remained neutral. "Is there something you want to tell me? Mom was speaking in riddles, too." He must have heard the frustration in Shelly's voice.

"I just want you to be happy."

"Ethan makes me happy." She thought Ben sighed.

"What's your plan?"

"I'm not sure." She frowned, glanced around the room. Glass-fronted triage rooms filled most of the four walls, with space for a public door and a medical staff door, plus a handful of the hard, plastic chairs. Blue privacy curtains inside each triage room concealed the wheeled hospital beds and monitoring equipment. The antiseptic smell that defined the hospital filled her nose. The sound of beeping, crying, and muffled conversation reached her ears. She focused on all those things while Ben finished reviewing the charts, waiting for her to figure out her next steps.

She snapped her fingers. "I've got it. It's brilliant. You can help me!"

Ben's eyes narrowed. "How can I help you?"

"You're a much better witch than I am. You can help me craft spells to show Ethan how much I care. After all, what are friends for?" Relief flooded her now that she had a solution.

Ben cringed, his lips thinning for a moment, before he offered a half-smile.

She didn't understand why he appeared less than enthused. *He'd never bonded with Ethan, but why wouldn't he want to help me?*

CHAPTER FOUR

BEN

Ugh, the Friend Zone. Still. Why wouldn't I want to help my best friend? Gee, I don't know. Because she's going after the man who just broke up with her? Although, if Ben was honest with himself, he wouldn't want to help her go after any man who wasn't him. Not that he said any of that to Shelly. She was so excited; and he meant what he'd said. He wanted her to be happy. She deserved to be happy. He'd have to ignore the sinking feeling in the pit of his stomach.

"Of course, I'll help you."

With a squeal, Shelly grabbed him in a hug, the chart he'd been reviewing a welcome barrier between their bodies. If he was going to be in the Friend Zone, then he needed to focus on helping his friend. Just because Ben thought they acted more like roommates around each other didn't mean Ethan would be a bad guy for Shelly.

"Thank you, thank you, thank you," she said. "You won't regret it."

Her excitement infectious, he laughed. "I'm sure I won't. But you might." Ben wanted to eat the words when her smile slipped.

"What does that mean?"

Should he take Nick's advice to tell her how he felt? What if she dumped him as a friend and continued to try to win Ethan back? Then he'd lose everything.

"Ben? What does that mean?"

He shook his head. "I'm only teasing. You know the old saying... be careful what you wish for..."

"You just might get it," they completed in unison. It had been a joke since they were kids, waiting and waiting for their magic to manifest, only for Shelly to learn hers wasn't so controllable. She'd been inconsolable after several near misses where people had almost gotten hurt, including a ridiculous car accident when they were sixteen. She'd thought it would be hilarious to cast a spell to take control of Ben's car and then set up a game of chicken to freak him out. Except what had happened was she'd lost control of her own car – nothing responded to her, not the steering, the brakes, nothing. And they'd had a front-end collision.

Luckily, they were only in a parking lot, so the slow speeds meant neither were hurt.

But the thought that her misfiring magic could have had serious consequences shook her hard. She didn't try using her magic again for almost six months, finally tempted when she saw a cat stuck in a drain and didn't want to wait for help to arrive. Of course, by then, her parents were prepared to bind it when it misfired again. She and the cat were fine, but that was it for magic.

Her frown lines smoothed out and she grinned. "I'm not saying everything's perfect."

"Nothing's perfect."

"Exactly." She nodded. "But, Ethan and I… we had something… have something. Whatever. You know what I mean."

"I do." Ben wanted her to look at him the way she looked at Ethan, but he also understood that she wanted to make it work.

"Start in the morning?" She checked her watch. "Um, later in the morning, I mean. Text me when it's a good time?"

"Don't you have client stuff scheduled for tomorrow?"

"Nothing I can't work around," she responded vaguely.

"I'll need to grab some sleep once my shift is done, so let's say lunchtime? Ish? I'll text you." Plus, he needed to return an unexpected voicemail from Las Vegas. Chief Resident at a major metropolitan hospital? In Sin City? He hadn't been looking to leave town. In fact, he'd hoped to get the position there at Wildcrest Hospital; but they'd been awfully quiet about which resident would get the nod. And if it wasn't going to work out with Shelly— no, he wasn't giving up yet.

"Lunchtime-ish sounds good."

"Nick will be in Ethan's room soon with the discharge paperwork. You guys should be on your way in no time," Ben explained in his professional doctor voice.

"Thanks, Doctor Ben. For everything." She gave him another hug.

He didn't want to let her go, but released her when she stepped back.

"I'm looking forward to tomorrow," she said.

"Me too."

She walked the few steps across the linoleum, slid open the sliding glass door to Ethan's room, and finger waved to Ben before disappearing on the other side of Ethan's blue privacy curtain.

Ben's plan differed from hers. He would help her, like the best friend he was. But, while she hopefully began to see him in a different light, he'd also hope her plan failed completely. Then he'd throw caution to the wind and tell her how he felt.

CHAPTER FIVE

SHELLY

Sleep eluded her the rest of that night. Thus, Ben caught her mid-yawn when he opened the door to his house before she could knock.

"It's a good thing you aren't trying to sneak up on anyone," he said, stepping to the side to allow her room to enter. He smelled nice; she wondered if it was the sandalwood shower gel he liked.

"Your brothers aren't home?" she asked, not seeing their cars parked out front.

"They're both at work. Aaron started his new job today," Ben said to her before leading her toward the kitchen. She followed him through the foyer to the kitchen, marveling at the remodel. When the brothers bought this house, its cracked tile flooring, outdated kitchen, and stained gray walls needed serious TLC. In the past six months, they'd worked tirelessly on it. Now it was a masterpiece with dark laminate wood flooring gleaming beneath newly painted soft white walls and recessed lighting.

"How exciting! It's at the new realtor's office, right?" She sat at one of the high stools surrounding the new quartz-topped kitchen island. She glanced around for Ben's familiar, Cookie, but didn't see the calico beauty anywhere. Cookie may have been the reincarnation of one of Ben's long-ago ancestors, but she was still a cat who liked to nap during the day.

"Yep. I can't believe my kid brother got his realtor's license." Ben shook his head, his back to Shelly while he opened the stainless-steel refrigerator, brought out a bottle of white wine. He grabbed two long-stemmed glasses from the cabinet. "I figured we could use some liquid libation for brainstorming the spells to use."

Shelly clapped in delight. "Perfect. Ooh, is this that new Riesling you mentioned? The drier one?" She spun the bottle to read the description on the back.

"I picked it up the other day, was saving it for the right occasion."

The wistful tone of his voice caught her attention. She glanced up at him. He immediately broke eye contact.

"Did you want something to eat?" He faced the pantry next to the refrigerator, but she could see the tips of his ears turning red.

"What's up?"

Ben turned back around, now holding a bag of tortilla chips. "What? Nothing." He set the bag on the counter with a big smile. "Chips and salsa. I know they go better with margaritas."

"No, it's perfect," she told him, still off kilter though not sure why. Her chest tightened with the uncertainty and she refocused on her best friend instead.

Ben filled their glasses, tore open the bag of chips, and dumped a healthy amount of medium-spice salsa in a blue and white patterned porcelain dish before taking the seat beside her. He held up his wine glass.

"To finding the right spells," he said.

"To finding the right spells," Shelly repeated, mirroring his glass with hers. Then savored the wine as it slid down her throat like a, well, fine wine. Ah, there was a reason a crisp Riesling was her favorite.

"What were you thinking for this grand plan?" he asked before popping a chip into his mouth.

Her fingers drummed on the island. "I'm not sure. It's more that I know what I can't do."

"Well, right. No love spells. No increasing wellbeing spells." His eyes cut to her, a devilish smile playing on his lips.

Shelly gave him a shove. He pretended to almost fall from the stool. "Yeah, yeah. Smart aleck. Other than those two."

They sat in silence for a moment, thinking about what else they could do that would be effective without violating the witch's code. The coven followed the standard code of "Do what you like so long as you harm none." But, the definition of harm could be fluid, and they wouldn't want to inadvertently land on the wrong side of it. A meow came from a back bedroom. Shelly jumped to her feet.

"Is that my Cookie?" She headed down the short hallway to the front bedroom. "Cookie?" A meow greeted her seconds before the calico cat came into view, curled into a ball on Ben's bed. She slow-blinked at Shelly, who kneeled beside the bed, scratching behind the cat's ears. Cookie purred in response. "You should come out to sit with us later," Shelly told her and the cat nodded.

It was an odd, but interesting, fact that all familiars could understand all witches, but each witch could only directly communicate with their own familiar. That way they could act as the advisors they were intended to be for their assigned witch. Thus, Cookie's nod, since Shelly wouldn't be able to understand the cat's thoughts.

Ben's familiar, like her own, had appeared when his powers first manifested at puberty. Cookie was so sweet-natured, unlike Shelly's familiar. She inwardly chuckled, though make no mistake, she adored her fox, Rose, despite a bark that sounded like the fox was imitating a tiny, yappy almost-dog. Plus, Shelly was the only witch she knew with a fox for a familiar.

"Are you going to stay in there loving on Cookie all day, or are we getting to work?" Ben asked from the kitchen.

"I'm coming, I'm coming," she said, giving Cookie a final kiss before rejoining Ben, who was still eating chips as though she had never left.

"Any ideas?"

Shelly slowly submerged her chip in salsa. She then removed the chip so fast that she spilled some on the countertop. Her eyes gleamed. "Yes, actually. What's the main issue between me and Ethan?" She popped the chip in her mouth.

"Is this a trick question?" Ben answered with a raised eyebrow.

"No," she replied, indignant.

"Then I'm not sure."

"It's that he doesn't know what he has, right in front of him," she said in triumph. She'd figured it out.

Ben tilted his head. "That's the issue?"

"Yes! We're meant to be together, but he can't see it for some reason."

"It's tough when somebody can't see what's right in front of them," Ben agreed, downing the remainder of his glass of wine in one swallow.

"Exactly," she agreed. "We're looking for a spell to help

him see what's in front of him," Shelly continued, talking through her thought process.

Ben poured another glass of wine.

Shelly stood from the stool and paced in front of the counter. "We need a spell to open his eyes." She stopped. "Help to see what has been unseen," she said, trying to use the formal spell-casting language she was so bad at.

Ben laughed. "Ah, I get it now." He thought a moment. "I can do that; a combination of spells for awareness, focus, and increased intuition ought to do the trick. Shouldn't be too hard, to be honest."

"Too hard for me, though, right?" She teased him.

"Yeah."

Shelly rolled her eyes. "What ingredients do you need?"

Ben frowned. "We should make a list. I'm pretty sure I don't have everything we need on hand. We'll have to go shopping."

She grabbed a small pad of paper and pen from a drawer next to the pantry, then held the pen aloft, at the ready. "Okay, go."

"Frankincense and jasmine for increased intuition."

She scribbled these as Ben considered what else they needed.

"Crystals for focus. Probably citrine and carnelian are best."

Shelly nodded, though she couldn't even remember what a carnelian crystal looked like.

"Rosemary for focus, as well, and marjoram and poppy seed for awareness." Ben's tongue protruded slightly, something he'd done his whole life when he was concentrating. She hid her smile. "And, I think we'll be okay with just a white candle," he said, nodding as though completing some internal debate with himself. "That's it."

"Okay," Shelly agreed and handed him the list. "What do we need to buy?"

Ben's eyes bounced between the list and various points in the kitchen, no doubt visualizing where specific ingredients resided. "The crystals, frankincense, and jasmine."

"Time for a visit to the apothecary," she sang out.

Ben matched Shelly's smile. He loved her grandparents almost as much as she did, and they'd been the proud owners of the Wildcrest Wizardry apothecary for decades. "Time for a field trip," he agreed.

CHAPTER SIX

BEN

Spring in the desert varied little. Today, the sun shone in the cloudless afternoon sky, though the temperature was mid-60s. And it completely matched Ben's positive mood. Spending time with Shelly always brightened his day. He was glad they were able to get together more days than not, even with his busy hospital schedule.

By turning his head, he could see the top of hers as she walked beside him along the path to the apothecary. He resisted the urge to wrap his arm around her shoulder when she shivered.

"Are you cold? Do you want my jacket?"

Her head tilted up to meet his gaze and she smiled

crookedly. "And have it reach my knees?" She looked ahead again. "It's not that far of a walk."

"If you're sure."

"I am." She pointed toward the rocks off the side of the concrete sidewalk. "Did you see him?"

Ben peered but must have been too late. "See whom?"

She hurried a few steps ahead and looked down at the rocks, hands on her hips as she bent over a bit. "Aww, he must have gone back underground."

"Chipmunk?"

"I think so. They're so cute. I love that they live along this path."

Her infectious enthusiasm got to him. He couldn't count how many times they'd walked the half-mile to the apothecary on the sidewalk that ran alongside the wash, or dry creek for storm drainage, between his street and Wildcrest's small downtown. Yet, he knew that Shelly delighted in the desert wildlife – and occasional housecat – that they'd see.

"Thank you," she said.

"For what?" Ben asked, still searching for the chipmunk that undoubtedly had gone underground as she surmised.

"For helping me get Ethan back. I know you've never really liked him."

His neck flushed at her words. He thought he did a better job at hiding his feelings. He certainly hid other feelings well.

Her fingers touched Ben's arm. "I'm not trying to make you uncomfortable. I just… you know how much it means to me. You're a good friend."

Goosebumps rose along his arm where her fingers grazed. "Best friends," he responded, squelching the desire to pull her into his arms. Being relegated to the friend zone hurt, but the thought of losing her hurt more.

Shelly squeezed his hand, leaving it cold when she released. Was it his imagination that she held on longer than was necessary? Their eyes met for a long moment and then her steps quickened away from him.

His phone rang before he could hasten to catch her. She stopped when she heard him answer the phone. "Hey, Dr. Casey."

"Do you have a minute?" Dr. Casey Hayes asked.

"Of course," he answered eagerly. When the Chief of Staff of the hospital called, one made time; especially when one wanted to be promoted.

"I apologize for the delay in getting back to you, but I wanted to be the one to tell you." She exhaled audibly. "You should let Las Vegas know you're considering their offer."

"I'm not getting the Chief Resident position." He said it matter-of-factly to his boss, but frustration surged. He'd been certain this was his path, to stay with his family and friends.

Shelly's mouth twisted, matching Ben's.

"It's not set yet, but they're looking hard at another candidate," Dr. Hayes continued.

"Jason?"

"I'm not at liberty to say, but he would be a competitive candidate."

Ben could read between those bright lines. Dr. Jason Lawson, his fellow resident and pseudo-rival, was the front runner for the position he wanted. "I appreciate the call." Ben swallowed that sharp pang of disappointment and disconnected.

"That was Dr. Hayes?"

"Yep."

"Is she really giving the position to Jason?"

"Well, it's not her position to give," he reminded Shelly. "But, yeah, she told me to consider Vegas."

Shelly's eyes widened. "You're seriously considering leaving?"

He shrugged. "If I had a reason to stay…"

She rolled her eyes. "Oh, I don't know. Your parents. Your brothers. Your friends."

They resumed walking along the concrete path, the desert alive around them. Ben focused on the shrubs, birds, and lizards – tried to ignore that she didn't specifically list herself, but used the generic *friends* label. "We'll see," he finally told her.

As they exited the wash a few minutes later, the backside of the businesses on Main Street appeared before them.

Yes, their main drag was not-so-creatively named Main Street. Of course, that was decades ago, so you couldn't really fault the founders. Ben and Shelly came up behind the apothecary and walked between it and the grocery next door. Reaching the street, they turned to face the two-story beige stucco building. Actually, Shelly had informed him once that it was really taupe, not beige. Sounded good to him. All he knew was that it was stucco. In the desert, stucco abounded.

Wildcrest Wizardry catered mainly to tourists who wanted "spells" but those in the know could get real spell-casting ingredients – and a great latte. Or so said Shelly, who admitted she was addicted to them. The apothecary store was large and bright, with a sweet, gentle lavender scent, and very well-organized by types of ingredients and spell intentions.

It was mid-afternoon in March, so Ben didn't expect too many tourists. But there would be some, based on the tour bus parked out front. There were always a few people, hoping to get an inside scoop about the witches of Wildcrest.

Shelly reached the door before him and pulled it open, stepping aside so he could enter.

"Proof that chivalry isn't dead," he quipped as he stepped past her. Her laughter followed him in.

"Hey guys," a bubbly voice greeted them before the door could even whoosh closed.

"Hey Rebekah," Shelly responded, wrapping the tall blond store manager in a quick hug. "Are my grandparents here?"

"They're at the post office checking on a delayed delivery. You'll probably miss them."

Even though the post office was only across the street, it was a small-town post office, with only Miss Jerri working. And, like every small-town cliché, she loved to chat with her customers.

"That's okay, I'll be back this afternoon."

Before he could ask Shelly why she was returning later, she'd hurried down the candle and crystal aisle. With a slight wave at Rebekah, who'd returned to the cash register, Ben followed Shelly.

"What do you think of this one?"

The sparkle in her eyes told him she was teasing, but he ignored that and took the dragon candle from her with mock-solemnity. "Yes, yes," he intoned. "This is perfect."

Shelly giggled.

He replaced the candle on the shelf. "I think we're good in the candle department."

She pointed to several rows of shining crystals. "Do you see the citrine and carnelian crystals?"

He watched her eyes scan the various crystals on display. Her mouth turned down at the sides for a moment as she searched. Ben wondered if she was thinking about how she struggled with crystal-based spells too.

"Here's a citrine," she said, handing him the yellow quartz before returning to consider the sparkling crystals.

He reached forward with his other hand, but she beat him to the stone he had just spotted.

"That's what a carnelian crystal looks like!" She gently lifted the palm-sized red-orange stone off the shelf, then turned the stone around.

"That's a beautiful choice," he said, his gaze on Shelly instead of the glassy, translucent crystal.

"It feels warm." She sounded surprised.

Her comment surprised him too, though really it shouldn't have. "Just because you have challenges controlling your abilities doesn't mean you don't have any," Ben reminded her. Shelly's look of gratitude elicited a flash of sadness for his best friend. Being a witch defined them. To be without that connection to their identity – he couldn't imagine.

They heard the sound of rubber soles behind them and then a hesitant question. "Excuse me?"

Ben turned toward the voice and found a middle-aged couple wearing matching outfits. Being completely honest, he liked tourists for their money, but also because they were fun to play with. Ben imagined it was like his familiar Cookie playing with a mouse. On second thought, that was kind of violent.

"Do you live here?" The female half of the couple looked between Ben and Shelly, trying to answer her own question. He returned the favor, inwardly chuckling at their yellow fanny packs and wide-brimmed floppy hats.

"We do," Shelly answered. "Can we help you?"

"Brian and I took the tour this morning," the woman continued. She, of course, referred to the bus tour that hit all the locations from *Witches in the Wild.* "This was the final stop, and they said you could get supplies for real spells here." On the word spells, her eyes widened, as if she couldn't quite believe what she was saying.

"You can," Shelly assured her, without a hint of irony. "That's what we're doing."

"No, you're not," the man disagreed. His stance, with hands jammed in the pockets of his cargo shorts, suggested the tour had not been his idea.

"Didn't you know that movie was basically a documentary? As in nonfiction," Ben told them. The woman's intake of breath confirmed for Ben she wanted to believe, but the man's expression soured.

"That isn't nice, making fun of the tourists," he said in a huff.

"Oh, Brian, they're not making fun of us."

Ben felt bad hearing the sincerity in her voice, and decided to try complete truth. "We're really not. Though I was joking about the movie," he amended his statement. "But witches do live here. It's just that nobody believes us."

Shelly shrugged when the couple looked at her for confirmation. "It's true."

"That's so neat," the woman said in a soft voice.

Her husband shook his head. "They're playing you, Jean."

Shelly placed a hand on Jean's shoulder. "I promise we're not." She leaned to whisper into the older woman's ear. Jean nodded along with whatever she was saying.

"Thank you so much," Jean enthused. "I'll try that." She pulled her husband toward an aisle with various dried herbs.

Ben narrowed his eyes at Shelly. "What did you tell her?"

"I just made a few suggestions for some herbs that could help improve his mood." She poked him in the chest. "And you know, since she doesn't have any actual power, that at worst, nothing will happen." She grinned. "But at best, the placebo effect will give them a lovely evening."

"Come on, Shelly," he said with his own small smile, before following the couple into the herb aisle.

Shelly quickly located the frankincense and jasmine, on the other end from where the tourists were peering at the choices. They exclaimed quietly to themselves after searching the internet on their smart phone. Ben assumed they were researching the magical properties of the items. He smothered a wider grin. Shelly was right. Let them have their fun. It was sweet of her to try to help.

Jean gave Shelly a little wave as the couple departed the aisle, the tourist clutching a handful of wide, flat beans.

Vanilla for love and as an aphrodisiac, if Ben had to guess. He wondered if he should grab some for him and Shelly. The impish thought arose before he could squash it. His mood instantly soured. If they brought any home, it would be for Shelly and Ethan, not him and Shelly, he had to remind himself.

CHAPTER SEVEN

SHELLY

On the walk back to the house, Ben was uncharacteristically quiet. At first, Shelly didn't realize he was providing monosyllabic answers, since she wasn't too talkative either, thinking about him leaving. It was different when they both left for college; they were on an adventure, together but apart. This time, the sense of loss… and he hadn't even left yet. It saddened her that she wouldn't see him all the time, and she wondered if that could be how he was feeling. "Is everything okay?"

"Of course."

"Are you sure?"

"Why wouldn't it be?"

"You've been quiet."

"I'm not allowed to be quiet?"

The guilty look on Ben's face following the comment suggested she must have looked wounded. And, indeed, his retort stung. She was only checking in with him, not criticizing. "You know you are," she said.

A desert rabbit caught her eye and she watched it start to hop away, then pause when it realized she and Ben were only about ten feet from it. Shelly halted; Ben walked another couple of steps before catching on and stepping back to her.

Shelly loved that her community had built itself around the desert like that, instead of bulldozing it all down for construction. The small wildlife flourished in these pockets of desert, especially the brown desert cottontails with the long ears. And the ears on the one they watched stood up straight, seeming a third the size of its narrow body. The rabbit eyed them, its white whiskers twitching. She wondered if it was deciding which was the bigger threat – the two of them on the sidewalk path, or the homes that lined the wash? In a dash, it raced away and disappeared, probably into an underground burrow among the rocks and shrubs.

"Sorry if I snapped at you," Ben said.

"Did something happen that I missed?"

A small sigh sounded. "Must be the tourists."

"Must be," she agreed, though really, she didn't. Since

when did the tourists rattle Ben? Confusion flared brighter. Maybe it was just the call from the chief, she decided. Ben would tell her how he was feeling when he was ready, because that's what best friends did.

They rounded the corner from the wash sidewalk and headed the final distance to Ben's green stucco house. She took a single step up the short three-step concrete staircase, and stood to the side of the turquoise door so Ben could unlock it. He shifted the apothecary bags from his right to his left hand.

"Do you want me to get those?" she asked.

"No, I've got them." He fumbled with his keys in his right hand and they fell to the concrete floor.

Too quick for him to object, she leaned down and snatched the keys off the floor. "Guess you need my help after all," she sang out.

Ben was still chuckling when they entered the house and headed straight for the kitchen. Standing side by side, they emptied the bags and lined up their supplies next to the arrangement they'd made before leaving.

"Do we have everything?"

Ben's warm eyes met hers and he placed his hand over Shelly's on the counter, giving it a gentle squeeze. "We have everything," he assured her.

Whatever weirdness had happened on the apothecary trip seemed to have dissipated.

"What do we do, oh wise one?" she asked.

"I'll walk you through it," he answered, and got to work. He lit the end of a small bundle of sage and waved it before him, cleansing the space of any negative energy. He blew it out when finished and they both inhaled deeply of the pungent aroma.

"First, I'll set our candles up for the directions." He placed four white votive candles in a diamond before him, intoning the power of the North, East, South, and West as he did so. He lit the candles then blew out the match.

"Now, I'll place our crystals in the sacred space." He placed the citrine crystal first near the West candle. "For detailed focus." The carnelian crystal he placed opposite, closer to the East candle. "To increase visionary focus."

"Now I'll mix our herbs together in the pewter bowl. This will allow their energies and purpose to intermingle." He placed a small amount of rosemary in the bowl. "First, the final ingredient for improving focus."

"Next, we'll add the frankincense and jasmine to increase intuition of what is before Ethan." Ben's fingers nimbly grabbed a pinch of the first and a dash of the second.

Shelly wanted to joke that she knew how to do spells, they just didn't work right for her. But she didn't. She enjoyed listening to his voice. Besides, interrupting a witch's spell-casting could be disastrous – even more so than her own disastrous magic.

"Finally, we'll add the marjoram and poppy seed for

awareness, so that Ethan may become aware of that which is before him." He reached for a spice, his hand hesitating. She almost broke her silence then, watching his hand hover there for a moment, before passing the spice by, and selecting a different spice, marjoram maybe. Or was that the poppy? She frowned when she realized she wasn't sure which he'd grabbed. Unusual for Ben to almost make a mistake like that. She started to ask what happened, but he was continuing the spell.

"Together, we'll focus on Ethan to receive that which we are sending. We ask you, Earth Mother, to show him a vision, to hear the unheard, help him learn what is before him, and give him the awareness to recognize its presence." Ben lit a match and set the concoction in the pewter bowl on fire. A crisp, woodsy aroma rose with flame as the herbs charred. He closed his eyes. "So mote it be." His eyes opened at the same time the fire extinguished.

"So mote it be," Shelly echoed, inhaling the lovely scent with its hint of sweetness.

Was that her imagination, or did a tingle race through her body?

Ben blew out the candles from West to South, at each one repeating, "We visualize the spark of the spell."

"Visualize Ethan and what you want him to see and understand," he instructed her.

She closed her eyes, surprised when she saw Ben's face instead of Ethan's. Mumbling under her breath, she asked the Earth Mother to show Ethan what she saw for him. A future with her. Shelly's eyes opened.

"Done," Ben concluded.

"Awesome, thank you."

"You're welcome," he said, meeting her gaze with an undefined look in his eyes.

"What's with the funny look?"

"I'm funny looking?"

"Seriously."

"Thinking about work, is all."

"Hmm, okay." She didn't push. He'd tell her about it when he was ready, though she wondered briefly if that was related to what happened after the apothecary visit, too. She checked her watch and gasped. "Is that the time? Ugh, I'm going to be late meeting Laura."

"Laura Harkin? I thought she didn't like you."

"She doesn't. I guess I'm that good," Shelly said with a big fake grin. "She wants me to redesign the coven's website."

"And you don't want to do it?"

She nibbled on her lower lip. "I'm reluctant to do it."

Ben chuckled.

"She doesn't like me," Shelly repeated his words. "Why would I want to work with someone who doesn't like me?"

"Why did you accept the job?"

"She's the head of IT for the coven's business, and I like the coven?"

"I'm sure that was part of it," he agreed.

"I need the work," she admitted.

"Is there a reason you can't do the job?"

"Nope." She knew where he was going, since this was the same process he used to help his medical students move through challenges.

"Then commit to doing the work," he said with a grin.

She gave a mock salute. "Yes, sir."

"Have fun. Check in with you later."

Shelly hugged Ben goodbye, his muscles hard underneath the medical school t-shirt. He must be working out more. She practically skipped to the car, excited to get through her meeting with Laura so she could be home when the spell opened Ethan's eyes and he saw what was right in front of him.

CHAPTER EIGHT

BEN

Ben watched Shelly slide into the driver's seat of her bright orange VW bug. She'd bought that neon monstrosity five years ago because it'd been on sale and looked lonely on the car dealership lot. A smile crossed Ben's face at the memory and he closed his front door.

Walking to the kitchen, his body betrayed him, teasing him with the lingering feel of Shelly against him in that final hug before she left. *What was I doing?*

Ben knew exactly what he was doing. A guilty flush crept up the back of his neck. His hand grabbed the spices off the countertop. Shelly had almost questioned him during the spell casting. He could see it in her eyes when he'd hesitated in selecting the next ingredient in the spell. She knew he didn't make mistakes like that.

But it hadn't been an almost-mistake.

"What are you doing, little brother?"

The deep baritone startled Ben. "Noah, what are you doing here?"

Noah Wright, Ben's big brother, was basically an older version of him. Their father's genes were clearly dominant. Noah offered a wide smile. "Left a document in my bedroom that I need for a meeting later." He gestured toward the front door. "Was that Shelly I saw leaving?"

"You know it was."

"I'd recognize that car anywhere." Noah opened the refrigerator. "Since I'm here, figured I'd have a quick snack. What were you two up to?"

"Now why would you think we were up to anything?"

Noah's eyes scanned the spices still on the counter. "That sure looks like a spell was being cast."

"You would not be wrong."

Noah laughed. "What did Shelly rope you into now? I heard about Ethan ending up in Emergency."

"Of course, you did." Ben replaced another ingredient in the cabinet. "Ethan broke up with Shelly last night." Ben hadn't meant to tell Noah, it just slipped out.

"I assume you immediately told her how you feel."

Ben's jaw fell open and the brothers' eyes met.

"Little brother, everyone in this family knows you've

got it bad for Shelly. You always have." He said this with ease, knife sliding through the apple on the plate before him.

"But, I never—"

"You don't have to."

Hopelessness surged, as he considered the implications of his feelings being so obvious to everyone but Shelly. "If all of you can see it, why can't she?"

"That would be too easy, right?"

Ben chuckled. "Yeah, I suppose."

"Am I to assume by your response that you didn't tell Shelly?"

Ben broke eye contact, gathered the remaining spices to put away. "The timing wasn't right."

"Why not?"

"Shelly has a plan."

"I'm sure she does." A slight scrape sounded and Ben turned to see Noah sliding onto a stool, preparing to eat the sliced apple and peanut butter before him, a smile playing on his lips.

"That's what we were doing. Casting a spell to get Ethan back."

"I know you aren't reckless enough to cast a love spell."

"Shelly's plan is to nudge Ethan back in her direction."

"That seems like something she would do. How'd you get dragged into it?"

"She asked." Ben sat on the stool next to Noah.

"You're helping her try to win back her ex?" He quirked an eyebrow. "I know Ethan's a nice enough guy, but they have zero chemistry. Please tell me you have another, secret plan that doesn't involve just waiting for her to come to her senses."

That flush creeping up Ben's neck increased. "Okay, that was my original plan."

Noah's laugh boomed around the kitchen.

"But I thought of a… different plan."

"Do tell."

"I realized while casting this afternoon's spell – to help him see what's right in front of him, by the way."

Noah snorted. "That's ironic."

"Anyway. I realized that my superior witch skills—"

"If you do say so yourself."

"—could come in handy," Ben continued, ignoring the interruption.

"How so?"

"I can cause her spells to backfire."

"And send Ethan to Emergency again? This doesn't seem like the wisest approach."

"No, no, not enough to hurt him. Of course not." Ben glared half-heartedly at his brother. "You can't honestly believe I'd do that."

Noah held up his hand. "I'm just teasing. Go on."

"I could cause the spells to go just enough wrong to be unsuccessful. Instead of doing X, it'll do Y. Though maybe not that precise. Similar to what happened when Shelly's spell did the opposite," Ben continued, thinking aloud about how to make the plan work.

Noah eyed Ben.

"What?"

"That's why you're red-faced. Feeling guilty that you're lying to the woman you claim to have feelings for."

"What? No!" The look of trust on Shelly's face flashed in his mind. Yeah, Noah was right. Not that Ben would admit that to him. "This is all for the greater good."

"You don't have to defend yourself to me, little brother. I think it's hysterical."

"So glad you're enjoying yourself."

"Thanks." Noah's smile slipped a fraction. "Just be careful."

"I am," Ben said with confidence, though felt shakier inside.

"If this goes sideways, I predict it will do so spectacularly."

"I told you, I won't do anything to harm Shelly. Or Ethan."

"That isn't what I mean."

"Yeah, I know."

CHAPTER NINE

SHELLY

Wildcrest Wizardry was both the apothecary and the best place in town to get coffee. Shelly loved the small coffee bar at the rear of the store. Not that she was biased at all, given that her Nana and Papaw owned it. She ran a hand along the top of the wood table before taking a sip of her latte. Her eyes kept straying to the door to the apothecary, making her unsure if choosing a seat with a direct sightline from the chair through the shop was the best choice.

"You need anything else, sweetie," a soft voice said at her ear before the owner came into view from behind her.

She smiled. "No thanks, Nana. I'm just waiting for a client."

Nana tilted her head, a lock of her short black hair falling over her eye. She swept it back. Shelly's neutral comment must have been said with an edge. Nana's purple eyes narrowed – a family trait that somehow missed Shelly's generation – and she frowned. "What client?"

"You'll see in about five minutes."

Nana set a blueberry muffin in front of her granddaughter. "To tide you over." With that, she returned to the counter, moving with the grace of a former athlete, which she was. And without magical enhancement. She was short and thin, like Shelly's mother, but had the wiry muscles of a runner. She still started every day with a two-mile walk before joining her husband and their store manager, Rebekah, to open the store and coffeeshop.

The air around her stilled and Shelly stifled a sigh. She might have misfiring magic, but even if she hadn't seen Laura, her finely attuned magical senses told her the redhead had arrived. Head held high, almost-genuine smile on her face, she stood to face her nemesis. Um, client.

"Shelly! So good to see you. Thank you for meeting me." Laura Harkin, probably six feet tall, short red hair slicked back, undoubtedly like some celebrity with whom Shelly was not familiar, and dressed in what certainly seemed to be an expensive fitted black sweater dress. Shelly wondered if Laura drove to Vegas to shop or if she was confident enough to buy online. Her magic gifted her the ability to manipulate matter in small amounts. Maybe she could reshape anything she bought to fit?

Shelly extended a hand which Laura gripped. "Of course. Always happy to meet with a potential new client." They sat across from each other, Laura placing her large handbag on the hand-carved wooden table between them. She rummaged within, pulling out her laptop and a pile of papers. Shelly recognized the initial ideas she'd emailed Laura.

Laura stared at Shelly, unblinking and unsmiling.

Audibly swallowing, Shelly wondered if that was a glint of satisfaction in the client's eyes, before chastising herself that Laura wasn't out to get her. She needed to bring it down a notch.

"Tell me about your ideas for the website," Laura demanded, pushing the pile of papers closer.

With a deep breath, Shelly jumped in. The designs for the coven website were fantastic, if she did say so herself. To the uninitiated, literally, it would just look like a Wiccan social club. And it certainly had aspects of one. But the initiated would have access to more magical coven business. Shelly had always found it amusing how the non-magical citizens in town knew, but didn't really know, they were surrounded by witches. Wildcrest was unofficially the country's most supernatural town. But not everybody believed, despite the movie and the Las Vegas resolution. They just enjoyed the money the tourists brought.

Laura nodded throughout the presentation. Shelly

found herself feeling hopeful that it wouldn't be as bad as she'd feared, trying to work with her frenemy (*did people still say that anymore?*) Then Laura opened her mouth.

"Generally, I like it. Just a few tweaks and it'll be there." She smiled, her cool blue eyes appraising. Like a shark.

And with that, the gloves came off. Shelly had never heard so many ridiculous demands. Laura wanted the colors changed a smidge on every page, every font choice. The photos were good, but not quite what she wanted, so she wanted all of them replaced. By the time she got to her complaints about the *Contact Us* form on one of the final pages, Shelly was ready to pull her hair out at the roots. Or Laura's. Didn't really matter.

But Shelly didn't. She even kept herself from sighing throughout the three-hour meeting. Yep. Three excruciating hours of being told that every single thing about the new coven website would need to be tweaked. She might have told Laura to shove it, and kept the money already paid for the initial concept pages, but she had friends in the coven. And they were ultimately paying Shelly an insane amount of money for this redesign. Beggars couldn't be choosers when a business was struggling. But Shelly thought she finally figured out why Laura hired her in the first place.

"You hired me just so you could torture me, didn't you?" Laura's eyes bugged at Shelly's question, and Shelly could have sworn she heard someone coughing to cover up laughter behind her at the counter. Her mouth dropped open to take back the question.

Laura recovered faster. "Why would you think that?"

She backpedaled. "Apologies. I misspoke. I'm still surprised you wanted to hire me for the job." Shelly couldn't believe how upfront she was being. "We weren't exactly friends in high school." Not that she'd ever really understood why Laura picked on her; she just knew the woman had done so for years.

Laura arched an eyebrow. "High school was over a decade ago. Some of us have moved on."

Shelly's face flushed.

Laura sighed. "You're the best in town," she said, her mouth twisting like she'd tasted something sour, "and the coven board of directors wanted to hire someone local."

"Of course." That explained the hire. And the attitude. But she'd need to be more careful. She couldn't just express how she was feeling like that, and risk crossing a line the coven board couldn't pull her back over from.

Laura snatched at the scattered pages remaining. "I think that's enough for today."

"I would agree, since we went over every page of the website."

Laura's blue eyes narrowed. "Sarcasm, really?"

"Of course not. Just clarifying why we were finished." Shelly offered an almost sincere smile.

Laura stood, towering in her stiletto boots, even after

Shelly scrambled to stand beside her. "I'll expect the redesigns tomorrow."

A response died on Shelly's lips. Her mind swirled with objections, but nothing she could say in polite company.

"You can accommodate, right? I'd hate to have to report back to the board that you can't." She smiled without showing teeth. "The initial designs are fine; you're just tweaking."

Shelly swallowed back an angry retort and went with sickly sweet. "That's absolutely no problem at all, Laura. Meet you back here tomorrow, same time?"

With a regal nod, Laura spun on her heels and strode away from the table.

Shelly reconsidered that Laura truly hated her. How could she possibly get the redesign done by tomorrow afternoon?

CHAPTER TEN

BEN

"When's the last time you two ate here?" Ben asked his parents and gestured at the trays on the plastic table. "Hospital food is not usually what people choose for lunch if they don't have to."

"Couldn't really say." Ben's father, Elijah, boomed out the statement. He didn't have an indoor voice. His patrician good looks drew attention anyway, but when he opened his mouth…

"That's not why we're here, of course," Ben's mother, Esther, added. Her long brown hair was done up in an elaborate hairdo – a French braid, he believed Shelly had explained once – with teal ribbons wound throughout. She wore no makeup, but her sparkling brown eyes and smooth skin didn't need enhancement, or so Shelly had also explained to him. These were his parents. He didn't pay attention to such things.

"You guys asked for this meeting." Ben lifted his eyebrows to prompt them to explain themselves. Not that he didn't enjoy spending time with his parents, especially for a break mid-hospital shift like this, but he hadn't gotten the impression this was purely a social call.

"You're spellcasting with Shelly to help her win Ethan back."

Ben sighed in the face of his father's statement. There was no point in asking how he knew. He was the High Priest of their coven, and that meant more than just leading the coven and its rituals. Ben didn't think his father could sense the energy from today's spell, but nothing happened in the coven that Elijah somehow wasn't aware of. "How do you know what the spell was for?" Ben asked instead as the question occurred to him. His parents exchanged a glance. "Noah."

"Noah," Elijah confirmed.

"He's just worried about you," Esther said and patted Ben's hand.

"Don't worry, I'm not angry at him. I know he means well." Didn't mean Ben wouldn't give Noah a piece of his mind later. Ben's phone buzzed. A number with a Vegas area code. He let it go to voicemail.

"Something the matter?"

"No," he answered his father slowly. "I've been approached by a hospital in Las Vegas to be their chief resident."

Esther looked stricken. "You're going to leave again?"

"I told them I'm considering their offer."

"I thought you got all that out of your system with college."

"Dad, it's not about getting stuff out of my system," Ben said.

"What about here?"

"I've been unofficially told that's off the table," Ben answered his mother's question. Esther and Elijah appeared nonplussed by that news. "Just wish me good luck. I haven't made a decision yet."

"Good luck," they dutifully replied in unison.

Ben's phone dinged an incoming text message. Shelly. "Excuse me a moment." He swiped the screen to read the full message.

"Everything okay?" Esther asked.

Ben laughed. "She just had a meeting with Laura Harkin. That went about as well as she'd expected."

His mother's eyebrows furrowed. "What happened? We asked Laura to hire Shelly for the website redesign." Esther Wright was the Chief Financial Officer of Wildcrest Witches International. Their witches' coven was incorporated, with employees and everything, so they could sell products through the apothecary and online. As CFO, Esther would have had a direct say in who Laura hired for the job. After all, while Laura was responsible for IT, at the end of the day, she answered to Esther.

"Laura has never much liked Shelly, for some reason. Since high school."

Ben's parents exchanged another glance, though this one he couldn't read. They'd been married long enough they spoke to each other through their eyes. He didn't think they were actually psychic though.

"What happened?" Elijah asked.

Ben relayed what the text said about Laura wanting changes to everything and the deadline for tomorrow afternoon.

His mother pursed her lips. "I'm sure Shelly can meet the deadline, but maybe—"

"I know you mean well," Ben interrupted, "but I don't think Shelly would appreciate if you intervened."

She laughed, a higher pitch than people usually expected. "She's a strong-willed one, that woman. And like a laser in her focus."

"That she is," Ben agreed. "Listen, I appreciate that the two of you are concerned about this, but you know me. Would I engage in irresponsible magic?"

An expression of surprise flashed on his father's face.

"What?" Ben asked. "Isn't that what this meeting is about? You want to caution me against using magic to help

Shelly win back Ethan." The table shook and he wondered if his mother just kicked his father to stay quiet. But he had no idea why she would do that. She spoke before he could ask.

"That's exactly why we asked you here," Esther agreed. Her hands wrapped around Ben's. "Just be careful, dear."

"Of course. Always."

Satisfied they'd gotten their point across, Elijah switched topics. Apparently, Shelly's grandparents were having trouble getting some rarer spell ingredients for the apothecary. Ben accepted the topic change, but felt off balance. He didn't know why else they would have called the meeting, if not to talk about maintaining responsibility with his magic.

CHAPTER ELEVEN

SHELLY

Ugh, this evening was so awkward. Shelly had been home for several hours working on the website changes Laura had requested. Shelly had purposefully sat at the apartment's dining room table instead of worked in hers and Ethan's shared office, and waited for him to come out of the guest bedroom. Her heart constricted at that thought. While she'd been out, he moved enough of his stuff to live out of the guest room these final days. But he hadn't come out of the bedroom. Not in hours. And there was an attached bathroom, so even that conspired against her.

A quick series of high-pitched barks drew Shelly's attention. Her fox familiar had been sitting at her feet.

Now she stood, staring in the direction of Ethan's room, the mask of dark fur around her eyes highlighting the image of her on alert. "What is it, Rose?"

Shelly couldn't read the fox's mind exactly, but they communicated through images and… well, magic. Rose was unhappy with whatever was happening behind the closed door.

"Should I go check on him?"

Rose tilted her head. If she could have rolled her eyes, she probably would have, her expression was so human-like. According to Shelly's father, her great-great-grandmother Rosalie, whose spirit had been reborn as the fox familiar, had been known in the family as a smart-aleck.

Heat suffused Shelly. Oh. Something was wrong. It couldn't be the spell. Ben had cast it and he never made spell mistakes.

Rose barked and stalked toward Ethan's door, her nearly-feline movements sleek and her body low to the ground. Shelly followed the fox, feet silent against the carpet. She put an ear to his door, but heard nothing. What had Rose so spooked? She was sensitive to cast magic, so the spell must be doing something.

Shelly tapped the tips of her fingers on the door. "Ethan?"

"I'm resting."

"Is everything okay?"

Silence.

She debated whether to knock again. Ethan's responses definitely weren't encouraging. Rose barked a third time. The fox even bared her thin, sharp teeth in displeasure. A squeak behind the door suggested movement on the guest bed.

The door cracked open. A bloodshot blue eye stared out.

"Is everything okay?" Shelly asked.

A barely perceptible grunt and Ethan opened the door the rest of the way. His pupils seemed off somehow. He blinked several times in quick succession. "Is everything okay?" he echoed. "That's a good question."

"It is?"

Ethan stepped past the two and headed toward the front of the apartment. Shelly followed mutely behind. He crumpled into one of the dining room table chairs, legs splayed, and dropped his head into his hands. She stared at the top of his blond head, then took the seat opposite him, closed her laptop so she could see him better, and waited. His muscles rippled under the black shirt he wore over khaki shorts as he inhaled deeply several times. He abruptly sat up and faced her.

"Ethan?"

"What do you see?"

Was that a trick question? "Um, I don't understand."

He ran a hand through his hair, gave his head a shake. He stared at her, unblinking. "Do my eyes look normal?"

"They seem a little bloodshot," she admitted.

He nodded.

"Are they bothering you?"

"Not exactly."

"Ethan, what is going on?"

Her stern tone did the trick and he answered. "I have tunnel-vision."

"Metaphorically or physically?" Was he seeing what was right in front of him? Just like the spell was supposed to show him. She squashed down a premature sense of happiness. It hadn't happened yet.

He looked at her askance.

She guessed it still wasn't happening. "Hey, that's a legitimate question."

He blinked rapid-fire several times again. "My vision has physically reduced down to tunnel vision. I can see what's directly in front of me, but my peripheral vision has vanished."

Oh no. A wave of nausea rolled through her. His words were almost word-for-word what the spell was supposed to do. But that wasn't the outcome she wanted. At. All.

Ethan looked at her, confusion on his face. "What should I do?"

"Um," she stalled. "Let me call Ben and see what he thinks."

The suggestion was actually pretty brilliant. As both a doctor and the spellcasting witch, he should be able to explain what was going on. And whether or not Ethan would need to visit the emergency room again.

CHAPTER TWELVE

BEN

The lift Ben felt when he saw Shelly's name on the caller ID vanished when she started speaking. He murmured in all the right places while she told her tale of woe. But he should have felt good. That was what he wanted. The spells to keep misfiring. At least he'd assured her that Ethan didn't need to go to the hospital. He knew that the tunnel-vision interpretation of the seeing-what's-right-in-front-of-you spell would be gone by morning.

"A whole day wasted," Shelly's voice said, loud in his ear. He removed the phone from the side of his head, considered the likelihood of being overheard in the janitor's closet, and put Shelly on speaker while he hopped into the small room and closed the door behind him in one fluid gesture.

"I wouldn't call the day wasted," he contradicted.

"Why not?" Shelly asked the question in a small voice.

His guilt flared. How could he answer? It wasn't wasted for him. "No, you're right. I'm just distracted by paperwork." The lie rolled easily off his tongue and the guilt turned to mortification. Was that what he was turning into? He never lied to Shelly before this week. Would the ends justify the means?

"Is now not a good time?"

"I always have time for you," he assured her. "You have my full attention."

"Thanks, Ben, I know you're always there for me."

He heard the smile in her voice and one formed on his face in response.

"But I just don't understand what happened. You did the spell, not me. This never happens to you."

"True," he agreed, for lack of anything else to say.

Shelly gasped and Ben bolted up from the sturdy white basket he'd been sitting on. The velocity of that motion caused him to bump his shoulder into a row of brooms and mops hanging on the wall. The "what?" in response to Shelly's gasp was drowned out by the cascading of those brooms and mops onto him in the small room.

"Ben, are you okay?"

He heard Shelly's question from the phone thankfully

still clutched in his hand and he brought it to his mouth. "I, um, might have made a tiny mess. I'm gonna put you on a shelf while I pick the mops and brooms up."

"You're gonna what… while you what…?" Now she laughed, full-bodied and genuine. "Thank you, I needed that."

"My clumsiness?" He hung a flat mop, sponge mop, and dust mop back on the wall, marveling that there could be so many varieties. "So glad I could entertain you."

She snorted.

Ben stilled. "Why did you gasp?"

"Right! Is it possible that my own misfiring magic somehow… infected yours?"

"No, I don't think."

"But it's possible."

"Anything is possible."

Shelly laughed. "We can always rely on my mother for a pithy saying."

"She's not wrong." Grace loved that particular phrase; if she had a catchphrase, that would be it.

"No, she's not," Shelly agreed. "Do you think it's possible?"

He hesitated, hand resting on the final dustpan.

"Ben?"

"I don't know if something like that is possible," he answered as honestly as he could, given the huge lie that started the mess. A bark sounded in Shelly's background.

"What does Rose say?" And could Rose sense his lying? Shelly's familiar seemed even more sensitive to the use of magic than Shelly herself.

"She's not sure."

Relief washed over Ben, followed by guilt that he felt relief. This was already ridiculous and they still had the rest of the week. "What's the plan?"

"After today's wasted day," she repeated and Ben let slide, "I'm no closer to convincing Ethan to stay with me. I still have Wednesday and Thursday. Maybe Friday morning, depending on when he's leaving."

She sounded so matter-of-fact, like this was a project with boxes she needed to check. He considered saying that and decided it didn't matter. In three days, this would be over, one way or another.

"The plan, then," she continued, "is to cast two more spells. Any ideas?"

"Let me think on it. Tonight's shift isn't quite as long. Meet at my place tomorrow morning around 10?"

"Are you sure I should be there? In case I'm right that my presence is interfering?"

He hung his head for a moment at her words, then recovered. "Not at all. We'll be especially careful tomorrow to counter any interference. I promise." The words nearly caught in his throat.

"Sounds great. Thank you so much, Ben. You're an awesome friend."

The call ended and he plopped back on the overturned white bucket. To be in the friend zone was bad enough, but what kind of awesome friend let someone he cared for take the blame for his actions? Ben cradled the phone, thoughts waging war in his head. It hadn't occurred to him that she would blame herself for his spells going awry. Making her feel bad hadn't been part of the plan. He was happy that Shelly was happy they were still going forward with the second chance of a spell. But the guilt threatened to overwhelm him.

This was all a lie. Even with the justification that it was for the greater good of helping Shelly realize she had feelings for him, what would happen if she found out before that?

He left the closet and resumed his shift. Those thoughts weren't helpful. He was in it until the bitter end. Now, he just needed to come up with another modifiable spell to misfire without sending Ethan into Shelly's arms, or the emergency department.

CHAPTER THIRTEEN

SHELLY

Shelly's eyes closed and she inhaled the rich scent of her mocha latte. The warmth through the cup almost too hot on her hands. Such pleasant sensa—

"Are you going to drink that thing or make love to it?"

Ben's voice cut through her reverie about coffee, and her eyes flew open at his word choice. "I'm totally going to make love to it."

The tips of his ears turning pink confirmed her zinger hit home. Of course, the flush she felt was a bit more unexpected.

"Do you know what spell you want to do?" He asked the question and turned toward the refrigerator. She watched him move a bunch of items around, but withdraw nothing. Curious.

"I don't know," she said slowly. "Maybe I should try a love spell after all."

That did the trick. Ben spun around, eyes wide. "Not a chance."

Laughter bubbled out. "I'm just teasing you."

"Do you want my help?" Ben leaned forward on the island.

"I do," she assured him, immediately contrite. "I was just trying to break whatever spell had you stuck in the open door of the fridge, rearranging stuff."

"Gee, thanks."

"What are friends for?"

"So, in all seriousness…"

"I had an idea for a spell," she finally answered his earlier question. "But, I'm not sure about it."

"What could possibly go wrong?"

"After sending Ethan to the emergency room, unable to breathe, and then causing his vision to narrow to pinpricks? Well, I don't know." She smirked.

"Let's hear it, then."

"What's happened so far," she started to recap instead. "My first spell was hit by my misfiring magic and we got the opposite. Trying to enhance feelings of wellbeing with saffron resulted in the opposite physical reaction. Trying to figuratively open his eyes to see what was right in front of him resulted in the loss of his peripheral vision for the day." She winced.

"What's wrong?" Ben interrupted her recap.

Tears filled her eyes. "I'm doing this to help Ethan realize his feelings for me before it's too late, but you should have seen him yesterday, Ben." She wiped the lone tear that broke free. "He was so scared and confused last night."

Ben came around the side of the island and gathered her into a hug. "It's going to be okay. This will work."

She wrapped her arms around his broad shoulders, accepting the offered comfort. The familiar sweet yet woody scent of his sandalwood shower gel wafted over her, increasing her sense of belonging. She leaned into the hug, tightening her grip on his shirt. A desire to kiss Ben flared.

What?!

She drew back with a shaky laugh, eyes on her latte. Suddenly, Ben's nearness provided an entirely different kind of warmth.

"Shelly?" His fingers burned her chin where they gently lifted her face so her eyes met his hooded ones. "What's wrong?"

"I..."

His fingers caressed her cheek. He leaned in. Her lips parted for the expected kiss. Disappointment surged when she felt a delicate kiss on her forehead.

Ben stepped back. He gave her the crooked smile that she loved. "We should get back to work."

"Work?"

"On the spell?"

"Right!" She had a goal. These odd feelings wouldn't interfere with that. She wouldn't let them. Would she? Should she? This was …confusing… but probably connected to all the misfiring magic flying around. If she stayed focused, she'd regain what was lost. That finally got her derailed thoughts back on track, so to speak. A wide smile split her face, confusing emotions and physical reactions placed firmly on the back burner. "My thought was to cast a spell to help Ethan regain what was lost. Me."

"Okay." Ben didn't look convinced. He sat on the stool next to her.

"We just need to work out the possible malfunctions to the spell and counter them ahead of time."

"Sure. What could go wrong?"

"Is that sarcasm?" Shelly asked with a laugh.

"Realism?"

Now they both laughed, the earlier awkwardness fading. "If the spell misfired like my original spell, then the opposite would be visited on Ethan."

"He'd lose what he has?" Ben asked.

"That's my guess."

"I'm imagining his car vanishing—"

"—his shoes disappearing off his feet—"

Ben gave a sly look. "Maybe he goes bald as he loses all his hair."

She doubled over with laughter, trying to catch her breath, the image of Ethan's luscious hair falling off his head. "This isn't a revenge spell."

"Maybe it should be."

"You'd never do that," she reminded her best friend.

He sighed. "No, I wouldn't."

"And if the spell misfired like the spell you cast to open his eyes to what's right in front of him, it would be taken literally."

"Lost items would be regained?"

"Yep. I envision every lost sock, key, mug magically appearing in the apartment by the end of the day." She snort-laughed.

"Depending on how careful Ethan has been over the years, your place could wind up looking like an episode of *Hoarders*."

"Oh, my goodness, that would be terrible indeed."

Ben belly laughed. "Even better – what if all his ex-girlfriends suddenly called, texted, emailed, or actually showed up." He widened his eyes in mock terror.

She playfully punched his arm. "Hey now, he and I have been dating for years. There better not be that many!"

"You never know how much of a player Ethan might have been in high school."

She frowned at the thought of her Greek god ex-boyfriend being a player.

"We're just joking around," Ben said.

"I know."

"Then why do you look like you sucked on a lemon?"

"Anyway, the point is we want to make sure we don't get something like either of these. Can you incorporate that into the spell?" She nibbled on her bottom lip.

"Yep. Not a problem. We're essentially doing a beacon spell, but narrowed in so that lost love is regained." He smirked. "And not other lost loves." Ben listed off the ingredients he needed, starting with the sage for cleansing and tobacco as an offering. "Lavender and passionflower for attracting love."

"Wait," she interrupted. "Isn't passionflower for friendship?"

"You are correct."

"Then?"

"Don't you want to be friends with your lover?"

"I didn't think about it that way." She stared at his back while he pulled his pewter set from the cabinet.

"That's what I'm here for." He flashed a quick smile. "And, finally, the dried rose petals."

As before, she had assembled the listed items on the island while he named them. Unlike before, just in case, she hovered over him watching closely.

"Shelly?"

"Yes, Ben," she answered, eyes still on the pewter bowl into which he'd begun depositing the ingredients.

"Look at me."

She did.

"Why are you hovering?"

"I'm being uber-careful."

"Are you now?"

She nodded.

"What exactly are you watching for? Not that I think it's what happened, but do you really think you'll be able to see your magic interfere with mine?" He quirked an eyebrow. He crushed the herbs together in the mortar, pressing and rotating the pestle to mix them completely.

"Point taken." She drank some lukewarm mocha latte.

He lit the mix on fire, intoning the spell under his breath. The fire extinguished with his final word, and he blew gently on the smoke, the commingled scent enveloping them for but a moment before lifting. "I'm finished anyway," he said with a dramatic sweep of his arm.

She giggled. "How come you aren't seeing anybody?" *Whoa, where did that come from?*

Ben's jaw dropped open.

In for a penny, in for a pound, as they said. "You're a great catch." And he was. She swallowed past the sudden lump in her throat.

Ben had an inscrutable expression on his face. "Guess the right woman hasn't seen me that way yet."

Her head tilted in confusion at his phrasing.

He winked.

Wait, was he *flirting* with her?

CHAPTER FOURTEEN

BEN

"I flirted with her, Nick. Flirted. And got bupkis." Ben continued trying to read the menu he held, but the words kept blurring. Good thing he didn't really need the menu. He and Nick were meeting for lunch in the local diner they'd eaten at a million times before.

The owner had renamed it Magic Eats after the movie exploded the town's popularity, but chose to keep the '50s décor, from the black-and-white checkerboard vinyl floor to the teal back-to-back booths along the front wall of windows.

"Tell me what happened."

He told Nick about leaning in, choosing not to kiss

Shelly on her delicious mouth at the last moment, and winking during his departure.

Nick chuckled. "You winked?"

The tips of Ben's ears felt warm. "Yeah."

"You definitely flirted."

"Thank you for agreeing with me."

"Just trying to understand the situation." Nick frowned. "But this was after you cast another spell on Ethan."

"It's not exactly *on* Ethan," Ben protested. "It's more *about* Ethan."

"To-ma-to, to-mah-to."

"The point is, I flirted with her and got no response."

"Maybe she needs to think about it?"

"What's there to think about? We almost kissed."

"But, you didn't."

"No, we didn't." Disappointment filled Ben. Again. "It's okay, though."

"It is?"

"This is all going according to plan." Ben's mood lifted when that realization hit. "No, she didn't respond. But the point was to help her see me as more than a friend over the course of this experiment. That's happening. By tomorrow, Friday at the latest, when Ethan is leaving, Shelly will realize she doesn't want him. Then I make my bold move."

A small cough reminded Ben that the two were out in public. He looked up at the waitress, an older woman with a bouffant hairdo who totally matched the diner's décor.

"Are you young men ready to order?"

"Yes, ma'am," Nick replied and ordered a Rueben sandwich on rye.

"And you?"

Ben ordered his usual pastrami with extra pickles on the side and they handed the waitress their menus. They looked at each other after she left.

Nick smirked. "I'm aware of that plan. Here's another way it goes down. She finds out you've been deliberately sabotaging the intention of the spells and never forgives you."

Ben's mouth went dry.

"You're playing with fire."

Ben fiddled with the napkin in his hands.

"You know what happens with most fires."

"People get burned. I know."

"Tell her the truth."

"What if I lose her friendship?"

"What if you gain her love?"

Ben's lips pulled down and he furrowed his eyebrows, before reminding Nick, "I flirted with her and got no response."

"That's the third time you've told me that. Are you sure you didn't get a response?"

The question stumped him. "She didn't say anything. She didn't kiss me."

"Neither did you."

"Hmm." He rewound the scene in his head and rewatched with an eye toward Shelly's body language. Did she lean into him a little bit? Was he correctly remembering that she closed her eyes? Did she want him to kiss her?

"And?"

"Well, dang. Now I'm not sure." Ben described what he thought he remembered seeing.

"You're so clueless. She wanted you to kiss her."

"You're certain?"

"As certain as I can be without being there to see it."

"That would be creepy."

Nick laughed. "You know what I mean."

"I do."

"What's the plan then?"

"I'm going to tell her how I feel." Mixed emotions swept through Ben at the decisive statement. The expected fear of losing Shelly, of course, but a growing ribbon of hope, too.

A single lifted eyebrow told him all he needed to know about Nick's confidence in his statement.

With renewed determination, Ben withdrew his cellphone and typed out a quick text to Shelly. *Dinner plans?*

Within seconds, her reply. *Wanna come over? Ethan's out tonight.*

See you at 7, he typed, then smiled at the phone when Shelly responded with a series of smiling emojis.

"That seems positive," Nick commented. Ben didn't look up in time to catch him, but wondered if he'd smirked when he said it.

"Dinner tonight at her place."

"You know what to do."

Ben nodded, unable to speak. After years of not knowing, tonight he would find out the truth. Either Shelly had feelings for him, or he was in the Friend Zone for life.

CHAPTER FIFTEEN

SHELLY

If Laura Harkin requested one more additional change, Shelly's moratorium on practicing magic was going to be rescinded. She did every single thing the woman had asked for, down to the minute detail, and here Laura was, criticizing all of it. Again. Shelly plastered a tight smile on her face.

"Anything else, Laura?"

Blue eyes narrowed in response.

Shelly guessed her tone wasn't as conciliatory as she'd hoped. "I want to make sure the coven is satisfied with the work." That, at least, was true. Laura might drive her batty, but her best friend's father was the High Priest and his mother the CFO of the business. Shelly wanted them to like it.

Laura's expression relaxed, ameliorated for the moment. She sighed. "Listen, Shelly, I'm not trying to be difficult."

An eyebrow raised of its own accord.

"I'm not," she insisted. She lifted a hand to get Rebekah's attention. The apothecary manager was acting as the coffee bar cashier today, apparently in addition to her regular duties. Despite the beautiful spring weather, there weren't many tourists here today.

"What can I get you?" the tall, bubbly blond asked when she reached the table.

"Mocha latte, right, Shelly?"

Surprised that Laura had paid attention to her prior order, Shelly simply nodded.

"And I'll take an espresso. Double shot, please."

Rebekah gave them a toothy smile and departed to make the drinks.

Laura moved as though to run a hand through her short red hair, then stopped herself. Probably didn't want to mess up that perfect style. "I know I'm demanding, but it needs to be done right." She lifted a single shoulder.

Shelly held her breath. The next statement better be just to work on this latest round of changes. Otherwise, she was going to be sorely tempted to say screw it to the huge paycheck, that struggling against Laura's increasingly impossible demands wasn't worth it.

"I think we're close."

Shelly's breath whooshed out at the statement.

"Did you know I hired your mother?"

"As a supernatural life coach?" Shelly asked in surprise.

"A little broader than that, but, yes."

"No, I didn't. She doesn't discuss her clients with me."

Laura nodded. "Of course, she wouldn't." A bright smile lit her face. "I love your mother."

"Um, me too?"

"She's been helping me understand myself more, to understand more the person I want to be. And be with."

Shelly had no idea why Laura would be telling her any of that.

"I can tell you're wondering why I'm telling you this."

Shelly's face warmed with a flush. The perils of having zero poker face. "To be honest, yeah."

"Grace and Robert have a love for the ages."

A genuine smile broke open on Shelly's face.

"High-school sweethearts who stayed true to each other, through ups and downs, trials and tribulations," Laura continued, almost like she was talking to herself. "Everyone should have that, you know?"

Shelly nodded, tears suddenly threatening to fill her eyes. "Yes, they should."

"They never gave up on true love."

Rebekah approached the table with their drinks. Shelly appreciated the break. There was no reason for Laura to be talking like that, except maybe it was Shelly's reminder of what to focus on. Her reactions to Ben this week were unnerving, to say the least, but Ethan was her one true love, and she couldn't give up on it. On him. That was the whole purpose behind the magic spells. She smiled at the memories of fun times with Ethan – visiting museums, hiking, watching movies – before her smile faltered as memories of times with Ben crowded in. Images of him bringing her soup when she had the flu. Calling to see how she did on her final exams. Offering support when she launched her new business.

Was Ethan really just a friend? No. Shelly knew from her parents that you only had one chance at true love, and hers was Ethan. After five years, it had to be.

Rebekah walked away and Shelly lifted her coffee, offering a wobbly grin for her frenemy, Laura. "To true love."

"To true love."

They both took sips, Shelly wincing at the heat from the freshly brewed beverage.

Laura stood. "I expect those changes by tomorrow." She strode off on her kitten heels.

Now that was the Laura that Shelly knew. But this time the demand did nothing to dampen her good spirits. She'd get the changes completed (again) on time because she was a professional. More importantly, she got the universe's hint. You never give up on true love.

Time to head home and see how that morning's spell went. Time for Ethan to regain his lost love. Her.

And, if she was more excited to have dinner with Ben first, well, that was just because he was her best friend. Right?

The universe needed to be clearer.

CHAPTER SIXTEEN

BEN

Boxes filled Shelly and Ethan's apartment, Ben noticed with satisfaction, then felt bad, knowing that hurt Shelly. He tried not to stare at how many of them there were while following her the short distance to the dining table.

Shelly gave him a half-smile. "I know how empty the apartment is looking."

"He's out for dinner?"

"I think he's at the gym?"

It surprised Ben that Shelly didn't know where the love of her life was tonight, but he fully intended to take advantage of the absence. His talk with Nick had clarified things. He'd tell her how he felt. He'd planned it out in his head; once they got through the initial pleasantries of dinner, he was laying it on her. And, hopefully Nick was right that she'd jump into his arms.

Shelly's small kitchen with the older white appliances was tucked off to the side after entering. Along that same wall was the dining area. The apartment designers had extended the linoleum from the kitchen to help designate it, but there were no walls or anything. She'd already set the table with her favorite turquoise tableware, that Ben had bought her when she graduated college.

"I hope you don't mind we're using the smaller forks and spoons," she said, her tone apologetic. The silverware looked designed for children when in his big mitts, but for tiny Shelly, using them was more comfortable.

"You know I don't," he assured her and slid into the seat at the four-top dark brown table, facing the kitchen.

Shelly hurried back toward a couple of pots and pans on the stove.

"What are you making? It smells delicious."

"I thought, for the beautiful spring we're having, that I'd go with something simple and light, so it's a vegetable pasta in a garlic sauce." She turned back to the stove.

Garlic sauce? Hmm.

Shelly lifted one pot and dumped its contents into the other. He watched colorful green, red, and yellow vegetables tumble into the pot of, presumably, strained pasta, probably linguine. Shelly loved linguine.

"Do you want some help?" He suddenly felt weird watching her finish dinner.

Her laugh filled the space. "I've got it." She then transferred the vegetables and pasta into a matching turquoise serving dish before carrying it the few steps to the dining table. She set the dish down on the table. "Let's eat."

They spent the next moments in silence, filling their plates with pasta. She'd also made a spinach salad and uncorked some white wine, which they now served themselves.

Shelly lifted her glass of wine and he mirrored the action. "To gaining clarity in our lives."

His heart stilled at her words. "To gaining clarity in our lives." Now was his moment.

"Shelly, I have something—"

"Wait until you hear—"

They both started and stopped at the same time, chuckling over the simultaneous speech. "Please, ladies first."

Shelly was practically beaming. "Wait until you hear what happened with Laura this afternoon."

"Given your smile, not what I would have guessed."

She shook her head. "Nope, not at all. I mean, yeah, at first it was the typical giving me a hard time nonsense. But, then…" She trailed off, bit her lower lip.

"Don't keep me in suspense," he teased.

"Laura began talking about my parents and true love."

His mouth felt like it was filled with cotton balls.

"My parents had their share of ups and downs, but it was all worth it, because they were high school sweethearts who recognized their one-and-only true love."

He opened his mouth to speak when she paused to take a drink of her wine. Then he closed it; he wanted to see where she was going.

"When Ethan dumped me on Monday, I questioned everything. And, working with you on the spells to win him back, I questioned again, and doubt crept in." Shelly leaned forward, face bright with excitement. "But when Laura started talking about my parents, something that had *nothing* to do with our business talk, I knew."

"Knew what?" Here it was. The moment of truth. She'd declare her feelings, he'd declare his, and they could finally get out of the Friend Zone.

"I knew it was the universe giving me a sign. Ethan is my true love. The doubt I'd felt was misplaced. I was confused—"

Shelly was still talking, but at her words, a roar filled Ben's mind and he couldn't hear her anymore. She'd had doubt. Maybe she was thinking about him differently? His body felt light, like a weight had been lifted. Not all of it, but some. She might be thinking about him differently. "I'm sorry, I missed that," he said when he realized that Shelly was staring at him intently.

"What do you think?"

He bit back the words he wanted to say. Nick would call him a coward later. But if that was what Shelly wanted. "I want whatever you want."

"My conversation with Laura reassured me that my plan to regain Ethan's love is the right one. Like my parents."

Ben nodded, crushed as that just-lifted weight crashed back into his body. His limbs, his stomach, his heart. But he didn't want to ruin her happiness. He guessed he'd read the signals wrong.

"What did you want to tell me?" she asked.

"What? Oh, nothing. Tell me how the rest of the meeting went with Laura," he deflected.

Shelly tilted her head for a nanosecond and he wondered if she'd challenge his non-answer, but she didn't. "I thought it was going horribly, but in the end it was good." She told him the details and he listened, thankful at least to be on another topic.

The front door opened, startling them. Ethan was home.

CHAPTER SEVENTEEN

SHELLY

A frisson of guilt surfaced when Shelly heard the front door opening. Unsure why she'd feel guilty having dinner with her best friend, she tamped it down, pushed back from the table, and hurried over to greet Ethan. And then slammed to a halt when she saw his face. Face flushed. Lips thinned into an angry slash. Eyes narrowed as if awaiting another attack. That didn't look good.

"Everything okay?" she asked.

Ethan brushed past her with a sharp nod aimed in Ben's general direction, and headed toward the guest room to the right.

"Ethan?" Shelly asked his retreating form.

He held up a finger, like he was asking her to wait, before entering the bedroom and closing the door firmly behind him.

She spun to face Ben, her eyes widened in distress. "What do you think happened?"

Ben had already stood at some point during the exchange with Ethan. Now he walked to her side and leaned in to whisper. "Give him a minute."

She nodded, hands flexing opened and closed while she stood there immobile.

Soon enough, the door reopened and Ethan stood in the doorway, his tall frame filling the space.

"Ethan?" Shelly asked again.

He seemed to deflate before their eyes, becoming physically smaller. He sighed and then trudged to the couch, collapsing onto the gray corduroy. His head dropped into his hands.

With a desperate glance at Ben, she moved to sit beside Ethan, wanting to comfort him, though not sitting close enough to touch.

Ethan lifted his head, his reddened eyes met hers. "I don't understand what's happening."

Now guilt filled her, and it was probably earned. "What do you mean?"

"The last few days… since you made me the dinner that sent me to emergency—" His eyes narrowed. "—I feel like I'm under attack."

"You just had an allergic reaction…" She trailed off, sputtering.

"Still. It all started there."

"All *what* started there?"

"Since that dinner, I've spent the night in emergency, had my peripheral vision vanish, and now, it started a few hours ago. The directions to a party I never attended when I was in high school popped into my head. That was weird, but I shrugged it off. Then, my brain began down the path, of all things, of a hiking trail I didn't take because I woke up that morning with the flu."

Ethan paused but nausea roiled Shelly's stomach. She knew what was coming, had figured out what went wrong with the spell this time. Guilt spiked higher and she wondered if this had all been a horrible mistake.

"The weird memories continued with greater speed over the course of that first hour. Do you know what all of them had in common?"

She shook her head.

"In every instance, they were for things I never actually did, for one reason or another. My head has been filled with directions, paths, you name it, for events I *never* did."

Oh, my Goddess, that was their fault. She risked a quick glance at Ben, could see the guilt telegraphed there. Her misfiring magic did that. She tainted Ben's magic with her own, and now Ethan was paying the price. Tears pricked Shelly's eyes.

"Somehow…" Ethan paused. "I don't know how…" He tried again without success. His empty eyes met her tear-filled ones. "All of this started with your dinner. I don't know how that triggered this, but whatever is going on…" Now his gaze took in Ben as well. "Stop it. Please, just stop."

"I don't know what you're talking about." The lie burned as it left her mouth.

Ethan shook his head. "You do. I don't know how."

Because I'm a witch! she shouted in her head. *And I'm a terrible one.*

He took her hand in his, the gesture not sweet. "I'm leaving Friday morning. Whatever started with that dinner needs to end. I'm sorry that it worked out like this, but…" He trailed off again, then released her hand.

Instead of reaching for Ethan to regain the contact, she looked at Ben, saw him standing next to the dining room table, his hands clasped in front of him. Only his expression belied the relaxed stance of his posture. And that broke her heart more. She dragged him into this. He wouldn't have done it for anybody else. She was certain of that. It needed to stop.

Ethan stood, his blue eyes taking in her first and then Ben. "I'm going to bed. Sorry to interrupt whatever was going on here."

Shelly and Ben watched Ethan cross the carpeted floor to the guest bedroom. He closed the door, almost gently this time. Maybe he'd already got his frustrations out. She scurried to her best friend's side, noticing he was still as stricken as she was about what had happened.

"He's right, Shelly."

"What do you mean?"

"It's over."

"It is?" Even though she'd had that thought, too, her irrational worry that she was losing her only chance at true love flared. Her stomach clenched.

Ben sighed. "It is." He embraced Shelly, comforting her as a few tears came loose and tracked down her cheek. That comfort of being in his arms, added to the knowledge that he would always support her, even following her into ill-advised hairbrained schemes, heightened her confusion. But Ben was her best friend. Pulling back, he stared into her eyes for a beat.

"Ben?"

"I'll talk to you tomorrow." With that, he released her and left the apartment before she could formulate a reply.

She returned to the dining room table, sat at her seat, surveyed the meal she'd made and shared with Ben. That brought a ghost of a smile to her face. She drank a large gulp of wine and considered the evening.

Ethan more or less guessed what had been going on – and despite herself, that impressed her – but the universe had given her a sign not to give up on her true love. If she stopped now, she would never know if she gave up too soon. Plus, then she wouldn't get to continue working with Ben on the spells.

A high-pitched bark disrupted her train of thought. Shelly met the fox's gaze and was shocked at the reproach she saw there.

"What?"

Rose barked again, shook her head, and slunk from the room.

Shelly swigged another drink of wine and made her decision. With a smirk and a nod at the Goddess, she declared her intention.

"This is the ultimate test of my loyalty and affection for Ethan. I get it. Tonight was rough, but I get it."

CHAPTER EIGHTEEN

BEN

Ben was glad the morning at the hospital had been quiet. It gave him time to think. He didn't get the chance last night to tell Shelly how he really felt, given Ethan's untimely and mood-killing entrance. Ben groaned. Ethan. It had been so much easier to think of him, even after all these years, as merely an interloper who would be mildly inconvenienced by the spells being cast. Seeing him in pain. Ugh.

First do no harm.

That was basically the primary tenet as both a doctor and a witch. And Ben had followed neither with Ethan. It wasn't as harmless as he'd told himself it was.

"Doctor?" The blond nurse called to him from the bed of their newest guest.

"Yes, Gretchen?"

"He's ready."

With a nod, he headed for the new admit and pulled the privacy curtain.

His phone began vibrating almost immediately. A quick check showed it was Shelly and although his heart sped up at the sight of her name, she'd have to wait until he was finished.

Gretchen and Ben worked seamlessly and quickly, yet someone, presumably Shelly, still texted or called three more times. He waited to confirm it was Shelly until he and Gretchen had finished with the patient and were back at the nurse's station.

"Someone really wants to reach you," the nurse joked as he scrolled through the notifications. Gretchen knew they weren't busy enough for it to be work-related.

He shrugged and offered a half-smile. "What can I say? I'm popular." Ben stepped away to the sound of Gretchen's chuckling. She had been a few years behind him in school, but he seemed to remember her always laughing.

The janitor's closet he'd hidden in before beckoned. A quick glance around the emergency department confirmed he had a few minutes. Shelly's last text had been, *Call me, please.* He assumed nothing bad had happened or she would have been explicit, but she still appeared desperate.

"Ben! Finally. Is emergency that busy?"

"Good morning to you, too, Shelly."

"Of course. Good morning, Ben." He heard the smile in her voice. "You have a minute now?"

"Maybe even two or three minutes."

"Excellent." He heard her take a deep breath. "I did some soul searching after you left last night."

His grip tightened on the phone. "And?"

"I want to try one last time."

"What? Surely I misheard you."

"You heard me just fine."

"Even though the spells have misfired?"

"Yup."

"Even though Ethan asked you to stop." He leaned his head against the closet wall, wanting to bang against it, but not wanting to cause brain damage.

"Yes."

He'd always thought it was only an expression, but he swore his heart fell with that single syllable. "I don't understand."

"I'm so glad you asked."

"I didn't really," he contradicted, but with a smile. Her excitement infectious as always.

"The Goddess sent me a sign with my conversation with Laura, so the spells misfiring and even Ethan's desire for all of this to stop, these are just tests of me. Tests of my belief in our true love."

A knife twisted in his belly at her words. She still thought Ethan was her true love.

"I'll admit last night almost caused me to give up. Look at it this way, Ben, today is the last day. We'll go out with a bang." She chuckled. "That hopefully doesn't blow Ethan up."

His mouth dropped open.

"Close your mouth, Ben. Yes, I know it dropped open."

"How do you do that?"

"You're my best friend," she said softly.

He stood from the upside-down bucket he'd perched on. Was that a hitch he heard on the last word?

"Will you help me with one final, pull-out-all-the-stops spell today? Ethan told me the moving van arrives in the morning. This is the last hurrah."

"Yes, Shelly, I'll help you with one final, pull-out-all-the-stops spell. After all, what are friends for?" He pulled the phone away from his ear at her happy squeal, smiling despite himself. "Lucky for you, this is a short shift this morning. Meet at my place at noon?"

"Let's make it one, I have another meeting with Laura, and it may go awhile."

He laughed. "Good luck."

"Thanks."

The call ended and he sat on the still-overturned bucket on the floor. An idea was formulating in his mind that would allow him to go through the motions of helping

Shelly, but still finally get off his butt and tell her the truth. He knew he wouldn't cast another "Ethan spell". But Shelly didn't need to know that. Yet.

Then again… he couldn't go through all of this to show Shelly he loved her, just to leave town for a new job. He pressed call on his phone.

"Dr. Ben, what can I do for you today?" Dr. Casey Hayes answered without preamble.

"What can I do to prove I'm the right resident to be Chief Resident?"

A low laugh sounded. "Are you turning down Vegas?"

"As soon as I hang up with you."

"Come to the board meeting today and tell them why they should hire you. I'll text you the details."

Ben thanked her for the recommendation and disconnected. That was the right decision. One phone call to Vegas would shut down that option. He was all in, personally and professionally. He hoped he didn't end up unemployed and still single.

CHAPTER NINETEEN

SHELLY

Shelly's meeting with Laura at Wildcrest Wizardry's coffeeshop couldn't have happened fast enough. She actually felt a pinch of anxiety when she sat at her favorite table. That was no good. At least she was a few minutes early, so she could relax with a mocha latte before Laura arrived.

"The usual?"

She turned her head at the sound of Nana's voice reading her mind, then smiled at the purple track suit that matched her grandmother's eyes. She must not have had time to change after her walk that morning with Papaw. At Shelly's nod, Nana hustled to the back to get the drink.

Clacking heels on the floor alerted Shelly to Laura's arrival before she saw her. Red hair slicked back per usual, blue eyes rimmed in dark liner. A cloud of some kind of light citrus fragrance clung to her. She set her bag on the table as she took the seat across from Shelly. "What do you have for me?"

"Hello to you, too," Shelly responded, but still pulled out her laptop. Rather than just mockups, she felt like they were close enough to go ahead and pull the site offline so she could institute the (hopefully!) final round of changes. And to be honest, she also thought if Laura saw them live, it would help her see how good they looked.

Laura frowned. "You already made the changes?"

Shelly bit back a sarcastic retort. "We seemed close to finished—"

"I make that determination, not you."

"Excuse me?"

"I am the client," she overenunciated, "so I make the determination of when we implement changes. Not you."

Speechless, Shelly could only stare at the redhead. A mocha latte appeared. If the look on Nana's face could kill, Laura would be a grease spot in the chair.

"Did you want anything?" Nana asked Laura, the sweetly saccharine tone enough to give everyone in the room cavities.

Laura flashed a not-quite-genuine smile. "Nothing for me. I won't be here long."

A brick formed in the pit of Shelly's stomach. She doubted Laura would fire her at this stage of the website redesign. But anything was possible.

With a curt nod, Nana turned and walked away.

"Show me what you've done."

At her direction, Shelly walked Laura through the implementation of the changes she'd requested yesterday. Laura made notes with every page, but said nothing. When they got to the final page, she made a few more scratches of pen on paper, and then sighed. That did it. Shelly snapped. "Why didn't you push back on hiring me? When Ben's mother suggested it. You don't even like me. This has to be as unpleasant for you as it is for me." She took a large swallow of coffee. That was completely unprofessional. What was the matter?

Laura stared impassively.

What the heck? She'd go for broke. "And speaking of that, why don't you like me?" Shelly pushed harder. "Since high school, you haven't seemed to like me, and I have no idea why." She heard the note of bewilderment in her own voice, and hoped Laura did too.

Laura sighed again, but this time she spoke. "I don't dislike you. Not really. Everything has always come so easy for you," she said, holding up her hand when Shelly opened her mouth to respond. "You asked. Now let me answer. Everything has always come so easy for you," she repeated, "and ...everybody... wants to be with you."

Her word choice baffled Shelly. "Everybody?"

Laura just shook her head.

"And you think everything comes easy for me? Do you know how much my new business is struggling?"

Laura's eyes widened.

"And—" Shelly couldn't believe she was about to admit this to her high school frenemy. "—do you know how much I suck as a witch?"

Laura covered her mouth with a hand.

"Are you laughing at me?"

"I'm not, I swear. I'm laughing at the situation."

Shelly quirked an eyebrow.

"I guess we never know what's going on with others."

"No, we don't."

"How much do you suck as a witch?"

"Is that rhetorical?"

"No." Laura smirked.

"Let's just say that when my magic matured, it didn't know how to manifest the right way," Shelly explained.

Laura looked confused.

"It has a tendency to misfire. Mostly to do the opposite of what I want."

"Can't you just cast spells with opposite intent?"

"It's not even consistent enough for that," Shelly groused.

"I suppose I can stop giving you a hard time," Laura said, her eyes twinkling.

"That would be nice."

"It's just tough."

"Not giving me a hard time is tough?"

Laura guffawed. "Did you know I had a crush on Ben in high school?"

Shelly ignored the whiplash caused by that conversation change. "What? Why didn't you ask him out?"

"He wanted someone else."

"That's news to me."

"Is it?"

Shelly tried to decipher the look on Laura's face and reviewed her years with Ben in high school. "I don't remember him being serious about anyone."

"Maybe he never got up the nerve to say anything."

"You'd think I would have noticed his interest in someone else," Shelly said, more to herself than Laura. This whole conversation was starting to feel deeper than expected.

Laura smiled. "The website looks great. Make it live and I'll let the board know, so they can take a look at it. They may want a few tweaks," she warned, "but probably nothing big."

"You already took care of that for them."

"Indeed." She gathered her papers to leave. "Say hi to Ben for me."

"Wait—" Shelly started to ask her what else she knew, but Laura swept past, clearly done with the conversation.

The comments about Ben perplexed her. Shelly was his best friend. How could she not know who Laura was talking about?

CHAPTER TWENTY

BEN

The employee lounge had only one person in it when Ben made a quick pit stop for some bad coffee before heading home to prepare for Shelly.

"Jason, you coming on or off?"

Dr. Jason Lawson, florescent lights reflecting off his bald head, offered a half smile. "Coming on. You leaving?"

"Yep. Just needed a little juice before I go."

Jason sidled up to Ben, leaned in conspiratorially. "I'm surprised you're leaving. A little birdie told me I should bring my A-game to the board meeting later today."

Ben refilled his travel mug with the swill disguised as coffee. "That meeting's not until 5 o'clock."

"You're the only other person who would be a serious contender for the Chief Resident position."

"I heard they're looking for a chief resident at one of the big hospitals in Vegas."

"Are they now?"

"That's what I heard." Ben took several steps toward the door, before turning back to Jason. "I'll see you later."

His response of, "I knew it," followed Ben into the hallway.

The sound of water greeted Ben when he walked through the front door of his house fifteen minutes later. He wondered what could be the source, before realizing one of his brothers must be home and taking a shower. Ben quickly changed in the bedroom before dumping dirty scrubs in the laundry room and heading into the kitchen. Shelly wasn't due for another half hour. He wondered briefly how her meeting with Laura was going. Better than last time, he hoped. But the break was good. It gave him time to prepare for the board meeting after.

The water from the back-bathroom shower stopped. Ben's plan for today's "spell" had come together nicely in his head. Time to implement. He gathered the spices and honey needed and laid them out across the island.

"Don't tell me you're still going through with your ridiculous plan," his brother, Aaron, said as he came into view from the hallway, his boots solid on the dark laminate wood floor. A shorter, stockier version of the men in their family, he had the same dark brown hair, but startling green eyes. Mischief danced in them right now.

"Did I ask for an opinion?" Ben responded. Aaron's blunt approach brought out Ben's sparring nature.

"I'm just trying to save you from yourself, brother of mine." He opened the refrigerator and pulled out sliced bread and a bunch of vegetables. Aaron's magic was an enhanced ability to communicate with animals; he'd become a vegetarian almost as soon as he could speak. Ben tried not to think about the implications of that.

Ben finished arranging the requirements for the "spell" and noticed Aaron frowning at what he had. "No comments from the peanut gallery, please."

Aaron shrugged and sat across from Ben to eat his veggie sandwich. Where Shelly usually sat. "When is she coming over?" his brother asked.

Ben checked his watch. "About fifteen minutes. She had a meeting with Laura Harkin first."

"Ooh, she's a she-devil, that one."

"She's not that bad. Very opinionated. Like you," Ben pointed out.

Aaron blushed and took a large bite of his sandwich.

"Strike a nerve?"

Aaron shook his head, appearing to concentrate on chewing and swallowing his food, before answering. "Stop being a weasel."

"I'm being a weasel?"

"Tell Shelly the truth."

"Again, not that I asked for an opinion, but I have a plan."

"Right. Noah told me. Help Shelly win back Ethan, and hope she falls in love with you in the meantime. How's that working out for you?" Another chunk of sandwich disappeared into Aaron's mouth.

Now Ben flushed. "That was the original plan. I'm trying something different today."

"Something connected to this hodgepodge you've got going on the counter?"

"I've been considering how to tell her, and I think I have the plan set."

Aaron unexpectedly threw up his hands.

"That was melodramatic."

"I needed to get your attention. You don't need a plan, other than to open your mouth and say the words, I like you, Shelly."

"It's not that simple."

"Good grief, man. Yes, it is. Why are you overcomplicating this?"

"I'm not."

"Uh-huh." Aaron brought his now-empty plate around the island to place in the sink. He gripped Ben's shoulder. "Now is your time. Don't screw it up. We've watched you pine for that girl for literally a decade. Now is your time," he repeated.

A knock on the door saved Ben from a reply. "Come on in," he called out.

Shelly walked through the door, her smile widening when she saw the brothers. "Hey Ben, Aaron."

Aaron and Shelly embraced and she chucked him on the shoulder. "Congrats on getting your realtor license."

"Thank you, Shelly. You let me know when you're ready to get a home of your own and I'll hook you up."

"You got it," she told him.

"I gotta run," he said to them. "You kids have fun. Don't do anything I wouldn't do." He stared into Ben's eyes, his expression serious. "Think about what I said, big brother." Without waiting for a response, he left.

Shelly turned, a question in her hazel eyes.

Ben sighed. "It's nothing. You know my brother has very strong opinions about everything. That he isn't afraid to share." But Ben wondered if his brother was right and he should just open his mouth and say the words.

CHAPTER TWENTY-ONE

SHELLY

Awkward energy floated all around the kitchen, but Shelly ignored it to take her customary seat at the island. She took a quick sip of her not-quite-empty mocha latte. "You ready to do this?"

Ben's mouth twitched. "You bet."

Quite the spread covered this part of the island. He'd laid out dried orange peel, wormwood, elderflower, and acacia, among several others she didn't immediately recognize.

"Gee, do you think you have everything you need?"

The tips of Ben's ears turned red.

"Is there something I should know?"

"How did your meeting with Laura go?" He focused on the ingredients before him, but if she didn't know better, he was randomly moving them around.

Hmm, interesting deflection. Alright, she would bite. Maybe it'd stave off some of the anxiety building in her chest. "It went really well, actually."

"That's wonderful. And a little surprising."

"I know, right?" She laughed. "In fact—" She eyed him shrewdly. "—Laura dropped a rather interesting piece of news. At least it was news to me."

Ben tilted his head. "I'm intrigued…"

"She said you had a crush on someone all through high school that you never revealed."

"Wha—" he stuttered, knocking over the salt. "Shoot." He turned to the counter behind him to grab a rag. If the tips of his ears turned any redder, they'd catch fire.

"You're a great guy. Why didn't you say something to her?"

Ben faced Shelly again, this time making eye contact that caused her to squirm in her seat. "What if she'd said no?"

"What if she'd said yes?"

Ben shook his head.

"Do I know her?" She asked the question lightly, but her heart hammered in her chest.

He opened his mouth to answer, closed it again.

"It's not a trick question." Her mouth had gone dry.

"Yes, you know her," he finally answered.

"Does she still live in Wildcrest?"

"Yes."

Butterflies had taken flight in her belly and she wasn't sure why they'd gone down that rabbit hole. That wasn't what they were there for. Ethan was her destiny. A sick feeling washed over Shelly at that thought, giving her pause. No, that was just the anxiety about missing her chance.

"You just had a whole conversation in your head, didn't you?" Ben asked.

She grinned to suppress that sick feeling, decided to focus on the task at hand. "Indeed." She surveyed the ingredients on the island again, now also recognizing Irish moss and nestle, and frowned. "What spell is this for? It seems… chaotic."

His eyebrows lifted.

"Did you not think I'd notice?"

"Well…"

"Hey," she protested. "My magic might misfire but I know what the spells are supposed to look like. And this doesn't look like anything. Or have you come up with something the world has never seen before?"

"No, you were right the first time. The ingredients aren't anything. There isn't a final spell."

"What do you mean? You couldn't think of one? I had a couple of—"

"No. I mean, I'm not casting any more spells to help Ethan realize he belongs with you."

A strange mix of sadness and elation arose. She pondered how that could be. Did she not want Ethan? Or was something else at play. "I don't understand," she admitted.

"Seeing Ethan last night, his misery." The look of anguish on Ben's face said it all. He'd decided that what they were doing was wrong.

"But I'm running out of time. This is my last chance." Even as the words left her mouth, she realized she was okay with that. That she was okay with losing Ethan. "Wait…"

"What?"

Shelly peered at Ben, saw guilt mixed with the anguish. "If I hadn't recognized this mess of nothing on the counter, would you have pretended to cast a spell?" A horrible thought occurred. "Have you been pretending all along?" Now Ben's entire face flushed bright red and she knew she'd hit home. "But there were consequences to the spells. I'm so confused."

"I wasn't pretending to cast spells." His eyes dropped to his hands gripping the island. "I was sabotaging them."

"Oh." Her stomach lurched and she leaned forward against the side of the island. "Why?"

Ben met Shelly's eyes and the anger there surprised her. "If Ethan can't recognize what he had in his relationship with you, then he doesn't deserve you. It's his loss."

"You lied to me," she said, voice flat despite the anger coursing through her.

"I did," he admitted. "Though not at first. When you asked me to help you, I fully intended on helping you with those spells. How could I ever say no to you?" He offered a half-smile and her expression softened.

"It's me." The words blurted out.

"Who's you?"

"Laura meant me when she said you had a crush on someone in high school." The lift she felt with that realization deepened her confusion. Ben was her best friend. Wasn't he? "I should have known. You're too good of a witch and my misfiring magic isn't strong enough to interfere."

He nodded.

"When did you start sabotaging—" Her eyes widened when she made the connection. "It was with the very first spell! When your hand hesitated over the ingredient. I knew something was off then. I just thought you almost made a mistake. But that was the exact moment you decided to change the spell outcome." If she wasn't already sitting, she would have collapsed. Her entire body felt weak with the realization.

"I'm sorry, Shelly." He started around the island and she bolted to her feet.

"No, don't come near me."

He stopped, dropped his hands to his sides.

"Why didn't you say something to me?"

"I didn't want to lose you," he whispered.

Hot tears filled her eyes and she blinked rapidly to forestall them falling. "That's unfortunate." She grabbed her mocha latte and work bag, clutched them to her chest like a physical barrier between them. "I don't ever want to see you again. Which should be easy, since you're going to Vegas anyway."

"Shelly, please—"

But she shook her head, already turning toward the front door. "No, don't." Her legs threatened to buckle as she made her way to the door that seemed miles away. "I don't know if I can ever trust you again." The door felt heavy in her grasp, but she swung it open. "Goodbye Ben." She slammed it shut. A wave of sadness crashed into her at the thought of never seeing him again.

CHAPTER TWENTY-TWO

BEN

Ben's eyes seemed glued to the front door. That Shelly just stormed through. That just slammed shut behind her. Slammed shut on them.

What had he done?

A noise behind him made him turn. Noah stood at the entry to the kitchen from the hallway, his expression sheepish.

"I didn't know you were home," Ben said.

Noah shrugged. "It seemed awkward to come out."

Ben sighed and sat in the seat vacated by Shelly, still warm from her body. "Yeah."

Noah took the seat next to him, put a brotherly arm

around his shoulder. "When I predicted this would go spectacularly sideways, I'd hoped I was wrong."

"I should have listened to my big brother's advice."

"Well, that's a given."

Ben stood up.

"What are you going to do?"

"I have no idea."

"At least she knows the truth now," Noah said. One corner of his lips lifted in a half-smile. "All of it."

Ben closed his eyes for a moment. "Not exactly how I'd hoped to spill my guts to her."

"No doubt."

Ben drummed his fingers on the counter.

"It's up to her if she can forgive you or not."

"She was pretty mad."

"That she was."

"Not that I blame her."

"That's good."

"You're being far too agreeable."

"No reason to kick a man when he's down," Noah said. "You know you screwed up. You also know it's out of your hands now." He slugged Ben's shoulder. "But, if I were a betting man, I wouldn't bet against you two lovebirds."

Hope flared. "Really?"

"Really."

"I guess there's nothing to be done but wait." Ben's brows furrowed. "What are you doing home in the middle of the day?" His older brother had also gone into medicine, in part because he had healing powers, but also because he liked doing old-fashioned home visits. He spent most days seeing patients in Wildcrest and the surrounding areas.

Noah grimaced. "I thought my healing energy would be enough for someone and it wasn't. A visit to the apothecary was in order. Since I was nearby, I came home to wrap up some chart notes." A wry smile replaced the grimace. "And then you trapped me in my room."

"Headphones before that?"

"Headphones before that," he confirmed.

"Sorry about that."

"No worries, little brother." He clapped Ben on the back. "Give her time. She'll come around."

The hope that flared earlier blossomed. "I hope so. This was why I didn't ever want to tell her," Ben griped.

"Don't even try that."

"What?"

"Are you seriously trying to equate lying to her about casting spells to regain her ex-boyfriend's affections with being honest about your crush on her for over a decade?"

"When you put it that way."

"You lied. She's angry."

"I thought you said you wouldn't bet against us?"

"I wouldn't. That doesn't mean you didn't royally screw up and that she won't need time to process what you did. And untangle her own feelings for you," Noah added.

"You know you're a general practitioner, not a psychiatrist."

"I know people."

"That you do." Ben waved toward the door. "You'd better get that medication to your patient."

With a jaunty salute, Noah headed for the door Shelly had slammed through. Was his brother right? Ben wondered if he needed to just give her time, or if he needed to do something to convince Shelly he was sorry and that they belonged together.

Despite the raging thoughts, Ben centered himself and headed back to the hospital for the board meeting.

* * *

"Welcome back, Dr. Ben," Jason Lawson greeted him with a smirk when he walked up to Jason standing outside the closed meeting room door.

"Thanks, Dr. Jason," he responded.

"Are you gentlemen getting along?"

The doctors turned at the sound of Casey's voice. The Chief of Staff strode toward them, shook their hands.

"I wish you both the best and think Wildcrest will do well with either of you as Chief Resident," Dr. Hayes said.

"Thank you, ma'am," Ben said.

"Ma'am? How many times have I said not to call me ma'am. I'm not that much older than you." Her brown eyes twinkled when she said it.

"Too many to count," he responded. Dr. Hayes looked

good for her age, whatever it was. A little heavy-set, no wrinkles, short curly brown hair cropped close to her scalp.

She entered the meeting room and spoke to them before closing the door behind her. "We'll get you in a moment."

The doctors waited in silence, standing in front of the door, uncertain. After about five minutes, Dr. Hayes brought Jason in, then Ben. The board asked a lot of questions about Ben's magical abilities. He assumed they did the same for Jason; Shelly had previously sensed magic in the other doctor, but neither of them could identify what it was.

Finally, the board asked the doctors in together. Ben and Jason stood side by side at the head of the table, around which the ten members sat. Several of them smiled at Ben, and his cautious optimism increased.

Dr. Hayes stood from her position on the opposite side of the table. "Thank you both for your applications for the Chief Resident position. It was truly a tough decision. You're both incredibly qualified and any hospital would be lucky to have you. However, there can be only one."

Ben swallowed. This was it. This was the moment. He held a breath to quell his jackrabbiting heart.

"Dr. Wright," she began, "we'd like to officially offer you the position of Chief Resident of Wildcrest Hospital."

"Thank you, Dr. Hayes, and board members," Ben said. "I accept the position. Thank you very much." A smile broke out on his face. He was staying in Wildcrest.

A chorus of congratulations came from the board members. Dr. Hayes addressed Jason. "We know you'll do well wherever you go."

"Thank you for that," he responded.

"Dr. Wright," she said to Ben. "Do you have a few minutes?"

"Of course," Ben said.

Jason turned to Ben with an outstretched arm. "Congratulations, man," he said as they pumped hands.

"Thanks. I'm sorry that throwing my hat in the ring last minute derailed you."

"It's all gonna work out for the best." He leaned in. "Looks like I'm moving to Vegas."

Ben boomed a laugh worthy of his father. "That's fantastic. And quick."

"I may have called them when you first mentioned it to me… and maybe followed up while you were interviewing to tell them you were off the market."

Ben's jaw dropped. "Wait, what?"

"I already knew you were getting it," Jason explained with a laugh. "They told me at the end of my interview, so it wouldn't come as a shock when they offered you the position. I asked if I could stay to congratulate you. And to add to the drama," he added with a wink. "When they brought you in for your interview, I figured why not make that call."

Ben shook his head at the audacity as Jason sauntered

away. Of course, Jason was right. The instant the board offered Ben the job, it wasn't even a question whether he'd accept. Except it was bittersweet. He was staying in town for a job he knew he'd love, but his reckless choices cost him Shelly.

CHAPTER TWENTY-THREE

SHELLY

Despite living in a small town, to drive from one end to the other still took twenty minutes, which was what Shelly had just driven from her apartment to her parents' home. They sounded thrilled she'd accepted their standing offer for dinner. She guessed she needed to do that more often.

Robert Newsome answered the door, smile on his face and wide-brimmed blue hiking hat barely covering his wild salt-n-pepper hair. No hair loss for her pop. He gathered his daughter up in a quick hug, then turned away.

"Your mother and I are making another donation. I've been going through my clothing," he called over his shoulder before disappearing around a corner.

"Hi, honey," her mother's voice came from the direction of the kitchen. Shelly's parents had bought their sprawling ranch-style home on the edge of town thirty years ago, when it wasn't the edge of town, but solidly in the desert. Time marched on, however, and the town caught up. It wouldn't get much closer. She believed her parents had purchased the surrounding few acres as well.

Shelly walked across the stone floor toward the kitchen, the smell of curry reaching her before she reached the space. "That smells amazing," she greeted her mother.

Grace Newsome took a few steps forward, dripping spoon in one hand and a cocktail in the other. She wore an apron with *Drinks well with others* emblazoned on it. That had been her apron for as long as Shelly could remember. She'd pulled her red hair into a messy bun and her purple eyes sparkled.

They air-kissed and Shelly sat at the large oak dining table across from where her mother stood at the stove.

"To what do we owe the honor?" Grace asked.

"I can't just have dinner with my parents?"

"Always. But we know you."

"Yeah." Shelly chewed on a cuticle while she delayed.

"Out with it, daughter."

Robert's voice from behind caught Shelly off-guard and she flinched.

He entered the room chuckling. "Not often I can sneak up on someone."

"I'm a little distracted," she admitted.

Her father grabbed a glass of water, patted her mother's bottom (*good grief*), and then sat at the table with Shelly. "What's going on, pumpkin?"

She fidgeted in her seat.

"Out with it," Grace ordered. "Isn't that why you're here?"

"I made a complete mess of things." To her horror, Shelly started to cry. Her mother turned the burner off and Shelly's parents moved to either side of their daughter. She managed to choke out the whole sordid story, right up to the point at which she stormed out of Ben's home.

"Ouch."

"Yep," Shelly agreed with her father.

"I wouldn't say you're the only one who made a mess of things," Grace soothed in her way, "but you definitely played a hand."

A laugh bubbled up. "That's helpful." Shelly bit her lower lip. "Can I save our relationship?"

"Anything is possible," her mother said cheerfully.

"Which relationship?" her father asked simultaneously.

Grace nodded at Robert before rising to bring dinner to the table. "Exactly."

"Which relationship?" Shelly repeated.

"What do you want?" her father tried to clarify.

"I'm conflicted." Shelly's gaze moved between her parents, still in love after all these decades. "I want what you have. True love." She sighed. "When you love someone, that's who you're with. You fight for that." Even as she spoke the words, Ben's image flashed in her mind. "I thought Ethan was my true love."

Her parents' expressions could best be described as stunned.

"What?" Shelly asked.

"Honey, that's a bit of revisionist history," Grace said.

"In what way?" Shelly narrowed her eyes.

"Do you think your mother and I were always together?"

"Well, yes."

They burst out laughing. "I was dating someone else when your mother and I met."

Grace smirked. "And I showed him what he was missing."

Shelly's eyebrows just about leapt off her face. "You broke up their relationship?"

"I wasn't with the right person," Robert defended Grace.

"Plus, we were young. Only in high school."

"Still." Shelly's mind reeled at the revelation. She had this entire love-at-first-sight, never-dated-anyone-else history for her parents, and it was a fantasy.

"Is that why you've been fighting so hard to make it work with Ethan?" Grace asked the question after sitting back at the table.

Both parents began filling their plates with food. Shelly sat like the proverbial bump on a log.

"We've been together for years," she said.

"Do you love him?"

She met her father's eyes. "No, I don't." With a shock, she realized that while she'd always liked Ethan – quite a lot, especially in the beginning – it was never love. She had been so hung up on the fantasy of her parents' story that she'd convinced herself she was in love with Ethan. And that because he was her one true love, she needed to do whatever was necessary to keep him. She wondered how she could have been so blind.

"Then you know what to do," her mother said.

"If you'll both excuse me," Shelly said, already rising from her seat. "I have to go."

If her parents responded, she didn't hear them, as she flew from their house to her car. She almost made a huge mistake. Several, in fact. Trying to win back a man she didn't love. Pushing away a man she—

The engine of Shelly's VW roared to life.

CHAPTER TWENTY-FOUR

BEN

A light knock on his door sounded. Ben wondered who that could be. He wasn't expecting anyone. Unfortunately.

The door swung open to reveal Shelly, cheeks flushed from exertion or excitement, long black hair braided down her back, hazel eyes confident.

Her appearance at his door shocked him. Ben's skin felt taut, nerve endings aflutter. Oh, man, he sounded like a romance novel. He guessed that was anxiety. "Come on in." He heard her footsteps follow, the door closing behind her, and they took their customary seats at the kitchen island. His heart sat lodged in his throat, waiting for her to speak.

Surely she wouldn't have come over to tell him again it was over. That meant—

"Hi Ben," she said softly.

"Hi Shelly. I'm glad you're here."

"Me too."

"Though, to be honest, I'm not sure what you want. You made yourself," he cleared his throat, "pretty explicit that you didn't want to see me."

She nodded. "I did. And in that moment, I definitely did not."

"In that moment?"

A shy smile formed. "That moment passed."

"I'm so glad." He took a deep breath. "Before you go any further, may I say something?"

"Have I ever been able to stop you?"

"That goes both ways, you know?" They chuckled and shared a knowing smile. Some of his uncertainty drained away. He considered what to say. "You're here either to say we're staying in the Friend Zone—"

Shelly snickered.

"—or you're here to say maybe you want to try for something more."

Shelly lifted a hand like she was going to reach out, then replaced it in her lap.

"I am throwing myself on the mercy of the court. You were right to be angry. I don't know what I was thinking." He paused to collect his thoughts. "No, that's not accurate.

I know what I was thinking. But I was in denial that it would end well." He gave her a crooked smile. "I've liked you since high school—"

"I've liked you too," she interrupted.

"Not like I've liked you."

"Oh."

"The timing was never right," he said.

She frowned and he could practically see her thinking through their years as friends.

"When you told me that Ethan broke up with you, my plan was to tell you then how I felt."

"But I ran roughshod all over that plan, didn't I?"

Now he gave her a wry smile. "That you did."

"Why did you agree to help me try to win back Ethan?"

His face flushed. "My initial plan was to help you, and hope it was unsuccessful."

"Gee, thanks."

"Hey, I figured you'd have so much fun with me, you'd realize you didn't want him."

An inscrutable look flashed across her face.

"Then, I decided to be more proactive."

Her lips thinned into a displeased line.

"And you were right to be angry. It occurred to me while casting that first spell that if the spells misfired just enough to be ineffective, it would minimize the possibility that Ethan would see the error of his ways." He quirked an eyebrow. "After all, you're awesome. That was the big flaw in the original plan. Guaranteeing he wouldn't come around."

"You really are a gifted witch," she said, a note of wonder in her voice.

"I don't understand."

"You not only crafted the spells, you altered them just enough to misfire, like my magic normally would, and without causing real damage. That takes skill."

Ben laughed mirthlessly. "Thanks? It feels weird being praised for something deceitful."

"Oh, don't get me wrong," she corrected him. "It was a bad choice. You just executed it very well."

"I figured modifying the spells to be sure they weren't successful would tip the odds in my favor. The rest of the plan was the same… at the end of the week, when Ethan left, I'd finally man up and confess my feelings."

"But I figured it out."

He shook his head. "I should have known you were too smart for me to fool for very long. I should have told you the truth, trusted in my feelings for you."

"That would have been a simpler option."

"I was scared."

"Of what?"

"Of losing you. Of losing your friendship if you didn't want more. I still am," he admitted.

Tears filled her eyes. "Ben."

Here it came. The moment of truth.

CHAPTER TWENTY-FIVE

SHELLY

What could Shelly say to Ben after everything he acknowledged? Her mouth opened and closed so many times, she felt like a fish. The look of expectation on his face broke through her paralysis.

"I remember how much fun we had in high school," she began.

"That's going back a bit."

"That's where it started, right?"

He wordlessly nodded.

"In high school, you were my best friend." She nibbled on her bottom lip. "And, I think you're right. I never thought of the possibility of more than that. As a scared teenager, frustrated with my misfiring magic, and unsure of myself… I probably would have run from you if you said anything."

Ben nodded again, no doubt pleased she confirmed his choice back then.

"College was its own little bubble. Fun, but I knew I wouldn't stay away." A rueful smile rose and fell. "We both know how much Wildcrest draws us."

"That we do."

"Being back, seeing you again." She swallowed against the lump in her throat. "I really liked Ethan, but if I'm honest, I came back to Wildcrest for you, not just for the town and my family."

Shelly sounded almost surprised when she acknowledged that, the truth having been buried so deep for so long. But Ben's intelligence, sweetness, and attractiveness – *how had I missed that?* – had always been there, waiting for her to wake up to them.

"You did?"

"But," she continued, her voice hard. "You almost blew it."

"I did."

"I agree that you didn't trust yourself – or me – enough to be honest. I accept that was a mistake." She half-smiled. "And I understand not wanting to ruin our friendship. When we conspired together to cast spells, it reminded me how much fun we have. Even in just the past few days, I began not caring as much about winning Ethan back. An eye-opening conversation with my parents—"

"Do tell," he said, quirking an eyebrow.

"A story for another day." She chuckled. "That conversation helped me realize my ridiculous inability to let go of Ethan had nothing to do with love. That missing spark wasn't because I was hiding being a witch. It was because it wasn't love. My relationship with Ethan was fun, and lasted longer than it probably needed to. But it was just fun, not love. That's why your betrayal hurt so much."

Ben cringed.

"Though I understand why you did it. And, really, was it so different than my decision to cast spells to win back Ethan?"

"I hadn't thought of it that way. You're as bad as me!"

"I am." They laughed. "We can both be better."

"We can," he agreed, his expression somber.

"And we need to apologize to Ethan," she said, wondering at the irony that she was finally going to tell Ethan the truth about her being a witch when she let him go.

"We will," Ben agreed immediately.

She took his hands, their warmth commingling. "Do you promise to never do anything like that again?"

"I do." His voice had become husky.

"You'll never lie, or otherwise deliberately withhold information from me?"

"Absolutely not."

"I wish you weren't going to Vegas."

An impish grin appeared. "Vegas isn't happening."

Her grip on his hand tightened. "It's not?"

"You're looking at the new Chief Resident of Wildcrest Hospital."

Shelly clapped with delight. "Congratulations! When did that happen?"

"A story for another day," he repeated her words with a smile.

"Would you like to have dinner with me?"

"Absolutely."

As if of one mind, they leaned toward each other, their lips touching lightly, then with more urgency. Energy zinged through them and she knew their magic was finding the other's. Maybe it was finally their time.

EPILOGUE

BEN

They took Shelly's VW bug to Ben's parents' summer barbecue and, as always, he was surprised how well he fit, given his height. On the opposite side of town from Shelly's parents' home, his parents built theirs on fifteen acres, allowing them unobstructed views of both the desert and the mountains. Shelly pulled through the open black wrought iron gates to the winding driveway.

After parking, they didn't enter the sprawling white ranch-style home with the red Spanish-style roof tiles. Instead, they walked around the side to join the others in the backyard. By the sound of it, quite a few people had beat their arrival.

"Happy Midsommer," Nick said, meeting them halfway across the large manicured lawn.

"Happy Midsommer," they echoed back. The celebration of Litha, or the summer solstice, always took place at Ben's parents' country estate, since his father was the High Priest of their coven.

Shelly checked her watch. "The ceremony is only five minutes away. Thank the Goddess we made it."

Nick walked with them toward the decorated folding tables pushed together in the middle of the lawn. Laden with fresh flowers, fruits, and vegetables, everything was in the summer colors of yellow, red, orange, and green.

"I'm so glad members of all the covens could make it out today," Ben said before taking a large bite out of the green apple he'd grabbed from the table.

Shelly pointed. "I'm going to say hello to Nana and Papaw." She took off toward her grandparents.

"Glad to see it's still working out with Shelly," Nick said. It had been a couple of months since their official first date and things continued strong with Shelly. Nick knew that.

"I know, I know. If I had listened to you to begin with." Ben shrugged and Nick laughed.

"There are your parents."

Ben spotted his father's head above a small crowd and moved toward him and his mother. Esther gave Ben a tight hug when he reached them.

"Son!" Elijah's voice boomed out. "You're just in time. We're about to start the ceremony."

With a nod, Ben stepped away from them, scanning the crowd for Shelly.

Elijah, standing next to the already lit candle at the makeshift altar, thanked everyone for being present. They called back their thanks to him for leading the ceremony.

"The sun shines from above, down upon the land and sea, makes plants grow and bloom," he began. All talking ceased when Elijah spoke.

Shelly found Ben, her fingers intertwining with his as they listened.

"Powerful sun, we honor you today, and thank you for the gifts you bestow," he continued.

Shelly's parents stood on the other side of the loose circle surrounding Ben's father. Grace's eyes were closed, Robert's arm wrapped around her shoulder.

"Known by many names, you nourish the crops, warm the earth, and bring life."

Shelly's fingers tightened on Ben's, and when he glanced at her, she gave him a big smile and nodded at something across the circle. He shifted his gaze and immediately understood Shelly's happy expression. Across the circle, Patricia, Shelly's younger sister, stood, feet planted apart, but slightly swaying to Elijah's words. She'd gone away for college, and stayed a little longer, getting some kind of graduate degree. Patty wasn't usually able to come home from Boston for ceremonies. Ben knew how happy her appearance made Shelly.

"The hope that springs eternal, we welcome you and celebrate your light, as we begin the journey once more into the darkness."

Smiles broke out across the faces of everyone in attendance with the last line. Although on the face of it, one would think the ending sad, but Wiccans celebrated the natural world, including moving through all the seasons.

"Hey, middle brother," a voice said.

Shelly hugged Noah the instant he reached them, Aaron only a step behind. "Hey, Wright brothers," she said, and giggled. That had been her running joke since high school.

Aaron's eyes cut to someone to the left behind the group, and Ben turned to see who had drawn his attention. He raised an eyebrow. "Since when does Laura Harkin attend the barbecue?"

Aaron flushed. "It's open to all."

"She's never attended before," Noah said, a small smile playing on his lips.

The three looked at Aaron, acutely aware of his nervousness.

"Okay, fine, I invited her."

"Ooh, you like her," Shelly said.

"No, it's not like that. She just hired me to help her find her own place."

"Uh-huh." Noah waggled his eyebrows at their younger brother.

"You know she and I have been friends since high school," he continued to protest. "I'm going to go say hello." With that, he made a beeline for the tall redhead.

Noah and Ben were talking about Aaron's new job, and who might move out first, when Ben noticed Shelly frown.

"Everything okay?" he asked.

Noah took that moment to excuse himself, and headed back toward the tables of food.

Shelly tilted her head, eyes glued to Aaron and Laura. "There's something about their magic that seems off right now."

Ben and Shelly tried to watch without staring, reading the other couple's body language. Laura stood about a head taller than the shorter, stockier Aaron. But Shelly was right, there was tension in their body language.

"I'm sure if Aaron needs our help, he'll let us know," Ben reasoned.

"You're right. I imagine we'll find out what's going on soon enough." She captured Ben's hand in hers and led him toward the party. "Let's go have some fun."

Don't miss Aaron and Laura's road to happily ever after in ***Love's Misaligning Magic (Wildcrest Witches, #2).***

THANK YOU!

Thank you so much for supporting my work and reading this book.

If you liked the book, please consider leaving a review online.

Just a few lines would be great. Reviews are not only the highest compliment you can pay to an author, they also help other readers discover and make more informed choices about purchasing books in a crowded online space. Thank you so much in advance.

If you didn't like the book or have concerns, please email me directly at
heather@heathersilvio.com

ABOUT THE AUTHOR

Heather Silvio mostly writes fun, flirty, fantasy romance and mystery to make readers smile. She sometimes strays from that to write non-supernatural fiction, and even the occasional nonfiction book. She is also an actress and licensed psychologist who channels her inner flapper as a 1920s jazz and blues singer when she isn't working.

Visit https://www.heathersilvio.com for more information and to sign up for her New Releases and Appearances Newsletter.